THE CASE OF
CHARLES
DEXTER WARD

CREATION ONEIROS

THE CASE OF CHARLES DEXTER WARD

H P LOVECRAFT

ISBN 978-1-902197-25-8

Published 2008 by Creation Oneiros

www.creationbooks.com

All world rights reserved

Copyright © Creation Oneiros 2008

Introduction copyright © D M Mitchell 2008

Cover picture: T-Weed

Design by Atavistic Images

CREATION ONEIROS

INTRODUCTION:

EXCAVATIONS – THE LYSERGIC DERIVE OF CHARLES DEXTER WARD

The Dreamtime of each town or city is an essence that precedes the form. The web of joke, remembrance and story is a vital infrastructure on which the solid and material plane is standing.
("Voice of the Fire", Alan Moore)

H.P. Lovecraft's work has at times been criticised for its lack of developed, 'believable' characters. Whether the criticism has originated from the pens of Edmund or Colin Wilson or Michael Moorcock (reactionaries both – pseudo-left or academic right) this negative appraisal has its roots in the narrow strictures of a 19th century positivist worldview or (at least) a 20th century humanist or 'social realist' one. At the end of the day these paradigms all boil down to the same illogical mass of bad faith which a post-modern sensibility can see as no longer relevant.

Viewed from a different (post-Nietzschean, post-humanist) perspective one can see that HPL's works in fact teem with a rich diversity of characters of incredible exuberance and a remarkable depth of character. However, rather than focusing on human beings as the determining characters in his work (and thus limiting the scope of his work to the social sphere and the changing fashions of politics and human affairs) the defining and motivating characters in Lovecaft's tales were the cities he loved.

Within the commonly held western paradigm of reality, cities (and landscapes by extension) are seen merely as backdrops against which Shakespearean or Dickensian dramas of human events unfold, extensions of human interest padding out a stage used purely for the enactment of human dramas of ego-aggrandisement. For Lovecraft, the city was decidedly not merely a set of parameters bounding human affairs, but an extension into space and time of the human psyche. In his writings the city also became a trans-human entity in its own right, sentient and strangely libidinous. In Lovecraft's City, individual humans are portrayed as mere facets and moving components; compartmentalisations of the 'hive-mind' of the city.

In Lovecraft's novel "The Case Of Charles Dexter Ward", Time is portrayed as more of a dynamic and defining, bounding factor than Space, although in reality the two are inextricably linked. At certain points in the story there is even a deliberate confusion – one being substituted for the other. As in Dunsany (obscurely) and Calvino (explicitly) the exotic location in which the tale is set is revealed to be in fact the familiar city, often the one of the reader's birthplace, extrapolated through time rather than space. Space is thus portrayed (as in Alan Moore's "Voice Of The Fire") as a secondary effect of the unravelling of **personal** Time. And human consciousness, unravelled in its fullness as 'culture' is embodied in the parameters of 'the City'. The manifestations of normally familiar objects, places and chains of events become monstrous as they are viewed stretching through time rather than in the customary spatial way. As the protagonist excavates layers of the city's memories and past, holes in time open beneath and around him. Eventually one of them swallows him. He merges with a past self and is obliterated. Later in the story, another character discovers hideous holes in a basement occupied by incomplete howling things; our human selves viewed extemporally, stretched along the time-grid.

In many ways, Lovecraft's tales are the precursor **and** the fullest logical development of the psychogeographical 'derive' (as seen in the early writings of Iain Sinclair and in Peter Ackroyd's "Hawksmoor" and "The House Of Dr Dee") in which characters drift aimlessly or purposefully through co-ordinates, spatial and temporal, of the landscape (usually urban) excavating layers of meaning and psychic relevance in ways pre-ordained on a personal or cultural level.

The city is organic, alive. The city, as distinct from the suburb (which is universal and uniform; there is, as JG Ballard has stated, only one global suburb which propagates itself like pond-weed in diverse locations simultaneously) emerges in different climes according to the genetic disposition of its inhabitants. It is capitalism with its empty assertions of individualism that produces the antithesis of the 'city'; the suburb. Uniformity suits the capitalist machine, which would ideally sell one book, one car, and one house – basically one product. And this omnipresent suburb is the antithesis of Lovecraft's ideal. HPL was in effect (and anyone who reads him closely will ascertain this) a lover of diversity. No wonder that his recurring deities were archetypes of chaos and complexity; Nyarlathotep (one of the most Nietzschean characters delivered to modern fiction) and Cthulhu (a primal 'female' symbol of the wild freedom of chthonic nature).

In Lovecraft the landscape is **always** sentient and totemic. Kadath in The Cold Waste, The Lost Plateau of Leng, Irem City of Pillars, Arkham, Dunwich, Innsmouth – and of course R'Lyeh! All of these have 'character' above and beyond the characteristics he daubed crudely on his human protagonists. This predilection is shared by modern writers like Ackroyd ("Great Fire Of London") and Moorcock ("Mother London") in the way they have portrayed cities as living organic 'entities'.

In "The Case Of Charles Dexter Ward", the events that unfold are tied inextricably with the landscape that Ward loves. In fact the narrative constitutes the dreaming mind of the sunset terraces unfolding through the prism of human awareness. What happens in this tale as happens in Dunwich or Innsmouth can be seen not only as inevitable (waiting for the presence of the right human agents through which to emerge) but also desirable in some larger scheme of non-anthropocentric events.

In the typical Lovecraft tale, the reader is co-opted, along with the protagonist, into a vicarious war with the 'modern world' and becomes involved in a search for a substratum – some 'fundamentalism' underlying the shifting sands of limited human values. The protagonist (and the reader) find that once they start digging, there is no bottom. There is no fundamental set of values, no 'universal system' – nothing onto which the conservative mammalian consciousness can cling except very tenuously and in voluntary ignorance. He (almost always 'he') becomes a diminishing figure in a landscape. The conservative rhetoric (often wandering into hysterical xenophobia) of most of the characters, and of HPL himself at certain periods of his life, can be seen as a hysterical reaction against the agoraphobic gulfs opening suddenly beneath their feet as a result of their misguided digging.

In Zoroastrianism playing with graves and memory are both forbidden, while one deserves a physical punishment, the other will bring eternal torment. Since playing with memory (i.e. inventing more lines of iteration through memory than mere remembering functions), sorcerously reinvents events not as localizable beings but deathless (in the sense of demonic restlessness) and inexhaustible germ-lines. Playing with memory outside of its remembering capacity enmeshes memory as a playground of agitated activities in the past which break the organizational consistency of the past in regard to present and future.
("Machines are Digging", Reza Negarestani)

5

THE CASE OF CHARLES DEXTER WARD

The essential Saltes of Animals may be so prepared and preserved, that an ingenious Man may have the whole Ark of Noah in his own Studie, and raise the fine Shape of an Animal out of its Ashes at his Pleasure; and by the lyke Method from the essential Saltes of humane Dust, a Philosopher may, without any criminal Necromancy, call up the Shape of any dead Ancestour from the Dust whereinto his Bodie has been incinerated.'

—Borellus

CHAPTER ONE

A Result and a Prologue

1

From a private hospital for the insane near Providence, Rhode Island, there recently disappeared an exceedingly singular person. He bore the name of Charles Dexter Ward, and was placed under restraint most reluctantly by the grieving father who had watched his aberration grow from a mere eccentricity to a dark mania involving both a possibility of murderous tendencies and a profound and peculiar change in the apparent contents of his mind. Doctors confess themselves quite baffled by his case, since it presented oddities of a general physiological as well as psychological character.

In the first place, the patient seemed oddly older than his twenty-six years would warrant. Mental disturbance, it is true, will age one rapidly; but the face of this young man had taken on a subtle cast which only the very aged normally acquire. In the second place, his organic processes shewed a certain queerness of proportion which nothing in medical experience can parallel. Respiration and heart action had a baffling lack of symmetry; the voice was lost, so that no sounds above a whisper were possible;

digestion was incredibly prolonged and minimised, and neural reactions to standard stimuli bore no relation at all to anything heretofore recorded, either normal or pathological. The skin had a morbid chill and dryness, and the cellular structure of the tissue seemed exaggeratedly coarse and loosely knit. Even a large olive birthmark on the right hip had disappeared, whilst there had formed on the chest a very peculiar mole or blackish spot of which no trace existed before. In general, all physicians agree that in Ward the processes of metabolism had become retarded to a degree beyond precedent.

Psychologically, too, Charles Ward was unique. His madness held no affinity to any sort recorded in even the latest and most exhaustive of treatises, and was conjoined to a mental force which would have made him a genius or a leader had it not been twisted into strange and grotesque forms. Dr. Willett, who was Ward's family physician, affirms that the patient's gross mental capacity, as gauged by his response to matters outside the sphere of his insanity, had actually increased since the seizure. Ward, it is true, was always a scholar and an antiquarian; but even his most brilliant early work did not shew the prodigious grasp and insight displayed during his last examinations by the alienists. It was, indeed, a difficult matter to obtain a legal commitment to the hospital, so powerful and lucid did the youth's mind seem; and only on the evidence of others, and on the strength of many abnormal gaps in his stock of information as distinguished from his intelligence, was he finally placed in confinement. To the very moment of his vanishment he was an omnivorous reader and as great a conversationalist as his poor voice permitted; and shrewd observers, failing to foresee his escape, freely predicted that he would not be long in gaining his discharge from custody.

Only Dr. Willett, who brought Charles Ward into the world and had watched his growth of body and mind ever since, seemed frightened at the thought of his future freedom. He had had a terrible experience and had made a terrible discovery which he dared not reveal to his sceptical colleagues. Willett, indeed, presents a minor mystery all his own in his connexion with the case. He was the last to see the patient before his flight, and emerged from that final conversation in a state of mixed horror and relief which several recalled when Ward's escape became known three hours later. That escape itself is one of the unsolved wonders of Dr. Waite's hospital. A window open above a sheer drop of sixty feet could hardly explain it, yet after that talk with Willett the youth was undeniably gone. Willett himself has no public explanations to offer, though he seems strangely easier in mind than before the escape. Many, indeed, feel that he would like to say more if he thought any considerable number would believe him. He had found Ward in his room, but shortly after his departure the attendants knocked in vain. When they opened the door the patient was not there, and all they found was the open window with a chill April breeze blowing in a cloud of fine bluish-grey dust that almost choked them. True, the dogs howled some time before; but that was while Willett was still present, and they had caught nothing and shewn no disturbance later on. Ward's father was told at once over the telephone, but he seemed more saddened than surprised. By the time Dr. Waite called in person, Dr. Willett had been talking with him, and both disavowed any knowledge or complicity in the escape. Only from certain closely confidential friends of Willett and the senior Ward have any clues been gained, and even these are too wildly fantastic for general credence. The one fact which remains is that up to the present time no trace of the missing madman has been unearthed.

Charles Ward was an antiquarian from infancy, no doubt gaining his taste from the venerable town around him, and from the relics of the past which filled every corner of his parents' old mansion in Prospect Street on the crest of the hill. With the years his devotion to ancient things increased; so that history, genealogy, and the study of colonial architecture, furniture, and craftsmanship at length crowded everything else from his sphere of interests. These tastes are important to remember in considering his madness; for although they do not form its absolute nucleus, they play a prominent part in its superficial form. The gaps of information which the alienists noticed were all related to modern matters, and were invariably offset by a correspondingly excessive though outwardly concealed knowledge of bygone matters as brought out by adroit questioning; so that one would have fancied the patient literally transferred to a former age through some obscure sort of auto-hypnosis. The odd thing was that Ward seemed no longer interested in the antiquities he knew so well. He had, it appears, lost his regard for them through sheer familiarity; and all his final efforts were obviously bent toward mastering those common facts of the modern world which had been so totally and unmistakably expunged from his brain. That this wholesale deletion had occurred, he did his best to hide; but it was clear to all who watched him that his whole programme of reading and conversation was determined by a frantic wish to imbibe such knowledge of his own life and of the ordinary practical and cultural background of the twentieth century as ought to have been his by virtue of his birth in 1902 and his education in the schools of our own time. Alienists are now wondering how, in view of his vitally impaired range of data, the escaped patient manages to cope with the complicated world of today; the dominant opinion being that he is "lying low" in some humble and unexacting position till his stock of modern information can be brought up to the normal.

The beginning of Ward's madness is a matter of dispute among alienists. Dr. Lyman, the eminent Boston authority, places it in 1919 or 1920, during the boy's last year at the Moses Brown School, when he suddenly turned from the study of the past to the study of the occult, and refused to qualify for college on the ground that he had individual researches of much greater importance to make. This is certainly borne out by Ward's altered habits at the time, especially by his continual search through town records and among old burying-grounds for a certain grave dug in 1771; the grave of an ancestor named Joseph Curwen, some of whose papers he professed to have found behind the panelling of a very old house in Olney Court, on Stampers' Hill, which Curwen was known to have built and occupied. It is, broadly speaking, undeniable that the winter of 1919-20 saw a great change in Ward; whereby he abruptly stopped his general antiquarian pursuits and embarked on a desperate delving into occult subjects both at home and abroad, varied only by this strangely persistent search for his forefather's grave.

From this opinion, however, Dr. Willett substantially dissents; basing his verdict on his close and continuous knowledge of the patient, and on certain frightful investigations and discoveries which he made toward the last. Those investigations and discoveries have left their mark upon him; so that his voice trembles when he tells them, and his hand trembles when he tries to write of them. Willett admits that the change of 1919-20 would ordinarily appear to mark the beginning of a progressive decadence which culminated in the horrible and uncanny alienation of 1928; but believes from personal observation that a finer distinction must be made. Granting freely that the boy was always ill-balanced temperamentally, and prone to be unduly susceptible and enthusiastic in his responses to phenomena around him, he refuses to concede that the early alteration marked the actual passage from sanity to madness; crediting instead Ward's own statement that he had discovered or rediscovered something whose effect on human though was likely to be marvellous and profound.

The true madness, he is certain, came with a later change; after the Curwen portrait and the ancient papers had been unearthed; after a trip to strange foreign places had been made, and some terrible invocations chanted under strange and secret circumstances; after certain *answers* to these invocations had been plainly indicated, and a frantic letter penned under agonising and inexplicable conditions; after the wave of vampirism and the ominous Pawtuxet gossip; and after the patient's memory commenced to exclude contemporary images whilst his physical aspect underwent the subtle modification so many subsequently noticed.

It was only about this time, Willett points out with much acuteness, that the nightmare qualities became indubitably linked with Ward; and the doctor feels shudderingly sure that enough solid evidence exists to sustain the youth's claim regarding his crucial discovery. In the first place, two workmen of high intelligence saw Joseph Curwen's ancient papers found. Secondly, the boy once shewed Dr. Willett those papers and a page of the Curwen diary, and each of the documents had every appearance of genuineness. The hole where Ward claimed to have found them was long a visible reality, and Willett had a very convincing final glimpse of them in surroundings which can scarcely be believed and can never perhaps be proved. Then there were the mysteries and coincidences of the Orne and Hutchinson letters, and the problem of the Curwen penmanship and of what the detectives brought to light about Dr. Allen; these things, and the terrible message in mediaeval minuscules found in Willett's pocket when he gained consciousness after his shocking experience.

And most conclusive of all, there are the two hideous *results* which the doctor obtained from a certain pair of formulae during his final investigations; results which virtually proved the authenticity of the papers and of their monstrous implications at the same time that those papers were borne forever from human knowledge.

3

One must look back at Charles Ward's earlier life as at something belonging as much to the past as the antiquities he loved so keenly. In the autumn of 1918, and with a considerable show of zest in the military training of the period, he had begun his junior year at the Moses Brown School, which lies very near his home. The old main building, erected in 1819, had always charmed his youthful antiquarian sense; and the spacious park in which the academy is set appealed to his sharp eye for landscape. His social activities were few; and his hours were spent mainly at home, in rambling walks, in his classes and drills, and in pursuit of antiquarian and genealogical data at the City Hall, the State House, the Public Library, the Athenaeum, the Historical Society, the John Carter Brown and John Hay Libraries of Brown University, and the newly opened Shepley

Library in Benefit Street. One may picture him yet as he was in those days; tall, slim, and blond, with studious eyes and a slight droop, dressed somewhat carelessly, and giving a dominant impression of harmless awkwardness rather than attractiveness.

His walks were always adventures in antiquity, during which he managed to recapture from the myriad relics of a glamorous old city a vivid and connected picture of the centuries before. His home was a great Georgian mansion atop the well-nigh precipitous hill that rises just east of the river; and from the rear windows of its rambling wings he could look dizzily out over all the clustered spires, domes, roofs, and skyscraper summits of the lower town to the purple hills of the countryside beyond. Here he was born, and from the lovely classic porch of the double-bayed brick facade his nurse had first wheeled him in his carriage; past the little white farmhouse of two hundred years before that the town had long ago overtaken, and on toward the stately colleges along the shady, sumptuous street, whose old square brick mansions and smaller wooden houses with narrow, heavy-columned Doric porches dreamed solid and exclusive amidst their generous yards and gardens.

He had been wheeled, too, along sleepy Congdon Street, one tier lower down on the steep hill, and with all its eastern homes on high terraces. The small wooden houses averaged a greater age here, for it was up this hill that the growing town had climbed; and in these rides he had imbibed something of the colour of a quaint colonial village. The nurse used to stop and sit on the benches of Prospect Terrace to chat with policemen; and one of the child's first memories was of the great westward sea of hazy roofs and domes and steeples and far hills which he saw one winter afternoon from that great railed embankment, and violet and mystic against a fevered, apocalyptic sunset of reds and golds and purples and curious greens. The vast marble dome of the State House stood out in massive silhouette, its crowning statue haloed fantastically by a break in one of the tinted stratus clouds that barred the flaming sky.

When he was larger his famous walks began; first with his impatiently dragged nurse, and then alone in dreamy meditation. Farther and farther down that almost perpendicular hill he would venture, each time reaching older and quainter levels of the ancient city. He would hesitate gingerly down vertical Jenckes Street with its bank walls and colonial gables to the shady Benefit Street corner, where before him was a wooden antique with an Ionic-pilastered pair of doorways, and beside him a prehistoric gambrel-roofer with a bit of primal farmyard remaining, and the great Judge Durfee house with its fallen vestiges of Georgian grandeur. It was getting to be a slum here; but the titan elms cast a restoring shadow over the place, and the boy used to stroll south past the long lines of the pre-Revolutionary homes with their great central chimneys and classic portals. On the eastern side they were set high over basements with railed double flights of stone steps, and the young Charles could picture them as they were when the street was new, and red heels and periwigs set off the painted pediments whose signs of wear were now becoming so visible.

Westward the hill dropped almost as steeply as above, down to the old "Town Street" that the founders had laid out at the river's edge in 1636. Here ran innumerable little lanes with leaning, huddled houses of immense antiquity; and fascinated though he was, it was long before he dared to thread their archaic verticality for fear they would turn out a dream or a gateway to unknown terrors. He found it much less formidable to continue along Benefit Street past the iron fence of St. John's hidden churchyard and the rear of the 1761 Colony House and the mouldering bulk of the Golden Ball Inn where Washington stopped. At Meeting Street – the successive Gaol Lane and King Street of other periods – he would look upward to the east and see the arched flight of steps to which the highway had to resort in climbing the slope, and downward to the west, glimpsing the old brick colonial schoolhouse that smiles across the road at the ancient Sign of Shakespeare's Head where the *Providence Gazette and Country-Journal* was printed before the Revolution. Then came the exquisite First Baptist Church of 1775, luxurious with its matchless Gibbs steeple, and the Georgian roofs and cupolas hovering by. Here and to the southward the neighbourhood became better, flowering at last into a marvellous group of early mansions; but still the little ancient lanes led off down the precipice to the west, spectral in their many-gabled archaism and dipping to a riot of iridescent decay where the wicked old water-front recalls its proud East India days amidst polyglot vice and squalor, rotting wharves, and blear-eyed ship-chandleries, with such surviving alley names as Packet, Bullion, Gold, Silver, Coin, Doubloon, Sovereign, Guilder, Dollar, Dime, and Cent.

Sometimes, as he grew taller and more adventurous, young Ward would venture down into this maelstrom of tottering houses, broken transoms, tumbling steps, twisted balustrades, swarthy faces, and nameless odours; winding from South Main to South Water, searching out the docks where the bay and sound steamers still touched, and returning northward at this lower level past the steep-roofed 1816 warehouses and the broad square at the Great Bridge, where the 1773 Market House still stands firm on its ancient arches. In that square he would pause to drink in the bewildering beauty of the old town as it rises on its eastward bluff, decked with its two Georgian spires and crowned by the vast new Christian Science dome as London is crowned by St. Paul's. He like mostly to reach this point in the late afternoon, when the slanting sunlight touches the Market House and the ancient hill roofs and belfries with gold, and throws magic around the dreaming wharves where Providence Indiamen used to ride at anchor. After a long look he would grow almost dizzy with a poet's love for the sight, and then he would scale the slope homeward in the dusk past the old white church and up the narrow precipitous ways where yellow gleams would begin to peep out in small-paned windows and through fanlights set high over double flights of steps with curious wrought-iron railings.

At other times, and in later years, he would seek for vivid contrasts; spending half a walk in the crumbling colonial regions northwest of his home, where the hill drops to the lower eminence of Stampers' Hill with its ghetto and negro quarter clustering round the place where the Boston stage coach used to start before the Revolution, and the other half in the gracious southerly realm about George, Benevolent, Power, and Williams Streets, where the old slope holds unchanged the fine estates and bits of walled garden and steep green lane in which so many fragrant memories linger. These rambles, together with the diligent studies which accompanied them, certainly account for a large amount of the antiquarian lore which at last crowded the modern world from Charles Ward's mind; and illustrate the mental soil upon which fell, in that fateful winter of 1919-20, the seeds that came to such strange and terrible fruition.

Dr. Willett is certain that, up to this ill-omened winter of first change, Charles Ward's antiquarianism was free from every trace of the morbid. Graveyards held for him no particular attraction beyond their quaintness and historic value, and of anything like violence or savage instinct he was utterly devoid. Then, by insidious degrees, there appeared to develop a curious

17

sequel to one of his genealogical triumphs of the year before; when he had discovered among his maternal ancestors a certain very long-lived man named Joseph Curwen, who had come from Salem in March of 1692, and about whom a whispered series of highly peculiar and disquieting stories clustered.

Ward's great-great-grandfather Welcome Potter had in 1785 married a certain 'Ann Tillinghast, daughter of Mrs. Eliza, daughter to Capt. James Tillinghast,' of whose paternity the family had preserved no trace. Late in 1918, whilst examining a volume of original town records in manuscript, the young genealogist encountered an entry describing a legal change of name, by which in 1772 a Mrs. Eliza Curwen, widow of Joseph Curwen, resumed, along with her seven-year-old daughter Ann, her maiden name of Tillinghast; on the ground 'that her Husband's name was become a public Reproach by Reason of what was knowne after his Decease; the which confirming an antient common Rumour, tho' not to be credited by a loyall Wife till so proven as to be wholely past Doubting.'

This entry came to light upon the accidental separation of two leaves which had been carefully pasted together and treated as one by a laboured revision of the page numbers.

It was at once clear to Charles Ward that he had indeed discovered a hitherto unknown great-great-great-grandfather. The discovery doubly excited him because he had already heard vague reports and seen scattered allusions relating to this person; about whom there remained so few publicly available records, aside from those becoming public only in modern times, that it almost seemed as if a conspiracy had existed to blot him from memory. What did appear, moreover, was of such a singular and provocative nature that one could not fail to imagine curiously what it was that the colonial recorders were so anxious to conceal and forget; or to suspect that the deletion had reasons all too valid.

Before this, Ward had been content to let his romancing about old Joseph Curwen remain in the idle stage; but having discovered his own relationship to this apparently "hushed-up" character, he proceeded to hunt out as systematically as possible whatever he might find concerning him. In this excited quest he eventually succeeded beyond his highest expectations; for old letters, diaries, and sheaves of unpublished memoirs in cobwebbed Providence garrets and elsewhere yielded many illuminating passages which their writers had not thought it worth their while to destroy. One important sidelight came from a point as remote as New York, where some Rhode Island colonial correspondence was stored in the Museum at Fraunces' Tavern. The really crucial thing, though, and what in Dr, Willett's opinion formed the definite source of Ward's undoing, was the matter found in August 1919 behind the panelling of the crumbling house in Olney Court. It was that, beyond a doubt, which opened up those black vistas whose end was deeper than the pit.

CHAPTER TWO

An Antecedent and a Horror

1

Joseph Curwen, as revealed by the rambling legends embodied in what Ward heard and unearthed, was a very astonishing, enigmatic, and obscurely horrible individual. He had fled from Salem to Providence – that universal haven of the odd, the free, and the dissenting – at the beginning of the great witchcraft panic; being in fear of accusation because of his solitary ways and queer chemical or alchemical experiments. He was a colourless-looking man of about thirty, and was soon found qualified to become a freeman of Providence; thereafter buying a home lot just north of Gregory Dexter's at about the foot of Olney Street. His house was built on Stampers' Hill west of the Town Street, in what later became Olney Court; and in 1761 he replaced this with a larger one, on the same site, which is still standing.

Now the first odd thing about Joseph Curwen was that he did not seem to grow much older than he had been on his arrival. He engaged in shipping enterprises, purchased wharfage near Mile-End Cove, helped rebuild the Great Bridge in 1713, and in 1723 was one of the founders of the Congregational Church on the hill; but always did he retain his nondescript aspect of a man not greatly over thirty or thirty-five. As decades mounted up, this singular quality began to excite wide notice; but Curwen always explained it by saying that he came of hardy forefathers, and practised a simplicity of living which did not wear him out. How such simplicity could be reconciled with the inexplicable comings and goings of the secretive merchant, and with the queer gleaming of his windows at all hours of night, was not very clear to the townsfolk; and they were prone to assign other reasons for his continued youth and longevity. It was held, for the most part, that Curwen's incessant mixings and boilings of chemicals had much to do with his condition. Gossip spoke of the strange substances he brought from London and the Indies on his ships or purchased in Newport, Boston, and New York; and when old Dr. Jabez Bowen came from Rehoboth and opened his apothecary shop across the Great Bridge at the Sign of the Unicorn and Mortar, there was ceaseless talk of the drugs, acids, and metals that the taciturn recluse incessantly bought or ordered from him. Acting on the assumption that Curwen possessed a wondrous and secret medical skill, many sufferers of various sorts applied to him for aid; but though he appeared to encourage their belief in a non-committal way, and always gave them odd-coloured potions in response to their requests, it was observed that his ministrations to others seldom proved of benefit. At length, when over fifty years had passed since the stranger's advent, and without producing more than five years' apparent change in his face and physique, the people began to whisper more darkly; and to meet more than half way that desire for isolation which he had always shewn.

Private letters and diaries of the period reveal, too, a

21

multitude of other reasons why Joseph Curwen was marvelled at, feared, and finally shunned like a plague. His passion for graveyards, in which he was glimpsed at all hours, and under all conditions, was notorious; though no one had witnessed any deed on his part which could actually be termed ghoulish. On the Pawtuxet Road he had a farm, at which he generally lived during the summer, and to which he would frequently be seen riding at various odd times of the day or night. Here his only visible servants, farmers, and caretakers were a sullen pair of aged Narragansett Indians; the husband dumb and curiously scarred, and the wife of a very repulsive cast of countenance, probably due to a mixture of negro blood. In the lead-to of this house was the laboratory where most of the chemical experiments were conducted. Curious porters and teamers who delivered bottles, bags, or boxes at the small read door would exchange accounts of the fantastic flasks, crucibles, alembics, and furnaces they saw in the low shelved room; and prophesied in whispers that the close-mouthed "chymist" – by which they meant *alchemist* – would not be long in finding the Philosopher's Stone. The nearest neighbours to this farm – the Fenners, a quarter of a mile away – had still queerer things to tell of certain sounds which they insisted came from the Curwen place in the night. There were cries, they said, and sustained howlings; and they did not like the large numbers of livestock which thronged the pastures, for no such amount was needed to keep a lone old man and a very few servants in meat, milk, and wool. The identity of the stock seemed to change from week to week as new droves were purchased from the Kingstown farmers. Then, too, there was something very obnoxious about a certain great stone outbuilding with only high narrow slits for windows.

Great Bridge idlers likewise had much to say of Curwen's

town house in Olney Court; not so much the fine new one built in 1761, when the man must have been nearly a century old, but the first low gambrel-roofed one with the windowless attic and shingled sides, whose timbers he took the peculiar precaution of burning after its demolition. Here there was less mystery, it is true; but the hours at which lights were seen, the secretiveness of the two swarthy foreigners who comprised the only menservants, the hideous indistinct mumbling of the incredibly aged French housekeeper, the large amounts of food seen to enter a door within which only four persons lived, and the *quality* of certain voices often heard in muffled conversation at highly unseasonable times, all combined with what was known of the Pawtuxet farm to give the place a bad name.

In choicer circles, too, the Curwen home was by no means undiscussed; for as the newcomer had gradually worked into the church and trading life of the town, he had naturally made acquaintances of the better sort, whose company and conversation he was well fitted by education to enjoy. His birth was known to be good, since the Curwens or Corwins of Salem needed no introduction in New England. It developed that Joseph Curwen had travelled much in very early life, living for a time in England and making at least two voyages to the Orient; and his speech, when he deigned to use it, was that of a learned and cultivated Englishman. But for some reason or other Curwen did not care for society. Whilst never actually rebuffing a visitor, he always reared such a wall of reserve that few could think of anything to say to him which would not sound inane.

There seemed to lurk in his bearing some cryptic, sardonic arrogance, as if he had come to find all human beings dull though having moved among stranger and more potent entities. When Dr. Checkley the famous wit came from Boston in 1738 to be rector of

King's Church, he did not neglect calling on one of whom he soon heard so much; but left in a very short while because of some sinister undercurrent he detected in his host's discourse. Charles Ward told his father, when they discussed Curwen one winter evening, that he would give much to learn what the mysterious old man had said to the sprightly cleric, but that all diarists agree concerning Dr. Checkley's reluctance to repeat anything he had heard. The good man had been hideously shocked, and could never recall Joseph Curwen without a visible loss of the gay urbanity for which he was famed.

More definite, however, was the reason why another man of taste and breeding avoided the haughty hermit. In 1746 Mr. John Merritt, an elderly English gentleman of literary and scientific leanings, came from Newport to the town which was so rapidly overtaking it in standing, and built a fine country seat on the Neck in what is now the heart of the best residence section. He lived in considerable style and comfort, keeping the first coach and liveried servants in town, and taking great pride in his telescope, his microscope, and his well-chosen library of English and Latin books. Hearing of Curwen as the owner of the best library in Providence, Mr. Merritt early paid him a call, and was more cordially received than most other callers at the house had been. His admiration for his host's ample shelves, which besides the Greek, Latin, and English classics were equipped with a remarkable battery of philosophical, mathematical, and scientific works including Paracelsus, Agricola, Van Helmont, Sylvius, Glauber, Boyle, Boerhaave, Becher, and Stahl, led Curwen to suggest a visit to the farmhouse and laboratory whither he had never invited anyone before; and the two drove out at once in Mr. Merritt's coach.

Mr. Merritt always confessed to seeing nothing really

horrible at the farmhouse, but maintained that the titles of the books in the special library of thaumaturgical, alchemical, and theological subjects which Curwen kept in a front room were alone sufficient to inspire him with a lasting loathing. Perhaps, however, the facial expression of the owner in exhibiting them contributed much of the prejudice. This bizarre collection, besides a host of standard works which Mr. Merritt was not too alarmed to envy, embraced nearly all the cabbalists, daemonologists, and magicians known to man; and was a treasure-house of lore in the doubtful realms of alchemy and astrology. Hermes Trismegistus in Mesnard's edition, the *Turba Philosophorum*, Geber's *Liber Investigationis*, and Artephius's *Key of Wisdom* all were there; with the cabbalistic *Zohar*, Peter Jammy's set of Albertus Magnus, Raymond Lully's *Ars Magna et Ultima* in Zetsner's edition, Roger Bacon's *Thesaurus Chemicus*, Fludd's *Clavis Alchimiae*, and Trithemius's *De Lapide Philosophico* crowding them close. Mediaeval Jews and Arabs were represented in profusion, and Mr. Merritt turned pale when, upon taking down a fine volume conspicuously labelled as the *Qanoon-é-Islam*, he found it was in truth the forbidden *Necronomicon* of the mad Arab Abdul Alhazred, of which he had heard such monstrous things whispered some years previously after the exposure of nameless rites at the strange little fishing village of Kingsport, in the province of the Massachussetts-Bay.

But oddly enough, the worthy gentleman owned himself most impalpably disquieted by a mere minor detail. On the huge mahogany table there lay face downwards a badly worn copy of Borellus, bearing many cryptical marginalia and interlineations in Curwen's hand. The book was open at about its middle, and one paragraph displayed such thick and tremulous pen-strokes beneath the lines of mystic black-letter that the visitor could not resist scanning it through. Whether it was the nature of the passage underscored, or the feverish heaviness of the strokes which formed the underscoring, he could not tell; but something in that combination affected him very badly and very peculiarly. He recalled it to the end of his days, writing it down from memory in his diary and once trying to recite it to his close friend Dr. Checkley till he saw how greatly it disturbed the urbane rector. It read:

"The essential Saltes of Animals may be so prepared and preserved, that an ingenious Man may have the whole Ark of Noah in his own Studie, and raise the fine Shape of an Animal out of its Ashes at his Pleasure; and by the lyke Method from the essential Saltes of humane Dust, a Philosopher may, without any criminal Necromancy, call up the Shape of any dead Ancestour from the Dust whereinto his Bodie has been incinerated."

It was near the docks along the southerly part of the Town Street, however, that the worst things were muttered about Joseph Curwen. Sailors are superstitious folk; and the seasoned salts who manned the infinite rum, slave, and molasses sloops, the rakish privateers, and the great brigs of the Browns, Crawfords, and Tillinghasts, all made strange furtive signs of protection when they saw the slim, deceptively young-looking figure with its yellow hair and slight stoop entering the Curwen warehouse in Doubloon Street or talking with captains and supercargoes on the long quay where the Curwen ships rode restlessly. Curwen's own clerks and captains hated and feared him, and all his sailors were mongrel riff-raff from Martinique, St. Eustatius, Havana, or Port Royal. It was, in a way, the frequency with which these sailors were replaced which inspired the acutest and most tangible part of the fear in which the old man was held.

A crew would be turned loose in the town on shore leave, some of its members perhaps charged with this errand or that; and when reassembled it would be almost sure to lack one or more men. That many of the errands had concerned the farm of Pawtuxet Road, and that few of the sailors had ever been seen to return from that place, was not forgotten; so that in time it became exceedingly difficult for Curwen to keep his oddly assorted hands. Almost invariably several would desert soon after hearing the gossip of the Providence wharves, and their replacement in the West Indies became an increasingly great problem to the merchant.

By 1760 Joseph Curwen was virtually an outcast, suspected of vague horrors and daemoniac alliances which seemed all the more menacing because they could not be named, understood, or even proved to exist. The last straw may have come from the affair of the missing soldiers in 1758, for in March and April of that year two Royal regiments on their way to New France were quartered in Providence, and depleted by an inexplicable process far beyond the average rate of desertion. Rumour dwelt on the frequency with which Curwen was wont to be seen talking with the red-coated strangers; and as several of them began to be missed, people thought of the odd conditions among his own seamen. What would have happened if the regiments had not been ordered on, no one can tell.

Meanwhile the merchant's worldly affairs were prospering. He had a virtual monopoly of the town's trade in saltpetre, black pepper, and cinnamon, and easily led any other one shipping establishment save the Browns in his importation of brassware, indigo, cotton, woollens, salt, rigging, iron, paper, and English goods of every kind. Such shopkeepers as James Green, at the Sign of the Elephant in Cheapside, the Russells, at the Sign of the Golden

Eagle across the Bridge, or Clark and Nightingale at the Frying-Pan and Fish near New Coffee-House, depended almost wholly upon him for their stock; and his arrangements with the local distillers, the Narragansett dairymen and horse-breeders, and the Newport candle-makers, made him one of the prime exporters of the Colony.

Ostracised though he was, he did not lack for civic spirit of a sort. When the Colony House burned down, he subscribed handsomely to the lotteries by which the new brick one – still standing at the head of its parade in the old main street – was built in 1761. In that same year, too, he helped rebuild the Great Bridge after the October gale. He replaced many of the books of the public library consumed in the Colony House fire, and bought heavily in the lottery that gave the muddy Market Parade and deep-rutted Town Street their pavement of great round stones with a brick footwalk or "causey" in the middle. About this time, also, he built the plain but excellent new house whose doorway is still such a triumph of carving. When the Whitefield adherents broke off from Dr. Cotton's hill church in 1743 and founded Deacon Snow's church across the Bridge, Curwen had gone with them; though his zeal and attendance soon abated. Now, however, he cultivated piety once more; as if to dispel the shadow which had thrown him into isolation and would soon begin to wreck his business fortunes if not sharply checked.

The sight of this strange, pallid man, hardly middle-aged in aspect yet certainly not less than a full century old, seeking at last to emerge from a cloud of fright and detestation too vague to pin down or analyse, was at once a pathetic, a dramatic, and a contemptible thing. Such is the power of wealth and of surface gestures, however, that there came indeed a slight abatement in the visible aversion displayed toward him; especially after the rapid disappearances of his sailors abruptly ceased. He must likewise have begun to practice an extreme care and secrecy in his graveyard expeditions, for he was never again caught at such wanderings; whilst the rumours of uncanny sounds and manoeuvres at his Pawtuxet farm diminished in proportion. His rate of food consumption and cattle replacement remained abnormally high; but not until modern times, when Charles Ward examined a set of his accounts and invoices in the Shepley Library, did it occur to any person – save one embittered youth, perhaps – to make dark comparisons between the large number of Guinea blacks he imported until 1766, and the disturbingly small number for whom he could produce bona fide bills of sale either to slave-dealers at the Great Bridge or to the planters of the Narragansett Country. Certainly, the cunning and ingenuity of this abhorred character were uncannily profound, once the necessity for their exercise had become impressed upon him.

But of course the effect of all this belated mending was necessarily slight. Curwen continued to be avoided and distrusted, as indeed the one fact of his continued air of youth at a great age would have been enough to warrant; and he could see that in the end his fortunes would be likely to suffer. His elaborate studies and experiments, whatever they may have been, apparently required a heavy income for their maintenance; and since a change of environment would deprive him of the trading advantages he had gained, it would not have profited him to begin anew in a different region just then. Judgement demanded that he patch up his relations with the townsfolk of Providence, so that his presence might no longer be a signal for hushed conversation, transparent excuses or errands elsewhere, and a general atmosphere of constraint and uneasiness. His clerks, being now reduced to the shiftless and impecunious residue whom no one else would employ, were giving him much worry; and he held to his sea-captains and mates only by shrewdness in gaining some kind of ascendancy over them – a mortgage, a promissory note, or a bit of information very pertinent to their welfare. In many cases, diarists have recorded with some awe, Curwen shewed almost the power of a wizard in unearthing family secrets for questionable use. During the final five years of his life it seemed as though only direct talks with the long-dead could possibly have furnished some of the data which he had so glibly at his tongue's end.

About this time the crafty scholar hit upon a last desperate expedient to regain his footing in the community. Hitherto a complete hermit, he now determined to contract an advantageous marriage; securing as a bride some lady whose unquestioned position would make all ostracism of his home impossible. It may be that he also had deeper reasons for wishing an alliance; reasons so far outside the known cosmic sphere that only papers found a century and a half after his death caused anyone to suspect them; but of this nothing certain can ever be learned. Naturally he was aware of the horror and indignation with which any ordinary courtship of his would be received, hence he looked about for some likely candidate upon whose parents he might exert a suitable pressure. Such candidates, he found, were not at all easy to discover; since he had very particular requirements in the way of beauty, accomplishments, and social security. At length his survey narrowed down to the household of one of his best and oldest ship-captains, a widower of high birth and unblemished standing named Dutee Tillinghast, whose only daughter Eliza seemed dowered with every conceivable advantage save prospects as an heiress. Capt. Tillinghast was completely under the domination of Curwen; and consented, after a terrible interview in his cupolaed house on Power's Lane hill, to sanction the blasphemous alliance.

Eliza Tillinghast was at that time eighteen years of age, and had been reared as gently as the reduced circumstances of her father permitted. She had attended Stephen Jackson's school opposite the Court-House Parade; and had been diligently instructed by her mother, before the latter's death of smallpox in 1757, in all the arts and refinements of domestic life. A sampler of hers, worked in 1753 at the age of nine, may still be found in the rooms of the Rhode Island Historical Society. After her mother's death she had kept the house, aided only by one old black woman. Her arguments with her father concerning the proposed Curwen marriage must have been painful indeed; but of these we have no record. Certain it is that her engagement to young Ezra Weeden, second mate of the Crawford packet *Enterprise*, was dutifully broken off, and that her union with Joseph Curwen took place on the seventh of March, 1763, in the Baptist church, in the presence of the most distinguished assemblages which the town could boast; the ceremony being performed by the younger Samuel Winsor. The *Gazette* mentioned the event very briefly. and in most surviving copies the item in question seems to be cut or torn out. Ward found a single intact copy after much search in the archives of a private collector of note, observing with amusement the meaningless urbanity of the language:

"Monday evening last, Mr. Joseph Curwen, of this Town, Merchant, was married to Miss Eliza Tillinghast, Daughter of Capt. Dutee Tillinghast, a young Lady who has real Merit, added to a beautiful Person, to grace the connubial State and perpetuate its Felicity."

The collection of Durfee-Arnold letters, discovered by Charles Ward shortly before his first reputed madness in the private collection of Melville F. Peters, Esq., of George St., and covering this and a somewhat antecedent period, throws vivid light on the outrage done to public sentiment by this ill-assorted match. The social influence of the Tillinghasts, however, was not to be denied; and once more Joseph Curwen found his house frequented by persons whom he could never otherwise have induced to cross his threshold. His acceptance was by no means complete, and his bride was socially the sufferer through her forced venture; but at all events the wall of utter ostracism was somewhat torn down. In his treatment of his wife the strange bridegroom astonished both her and the community by displaying an extreme graciousness and consideration. The new house in Olney Court was now wholly free from disturbing manifestations, and although Curwen was much absent at the Pawtuxet farm which his wife never visited, he seemed more like a normal citizen than at any other time in his long years of residence. Only one person remained in open enmity with him, this being the youthful ship's officer whose engagement to Eliza Tillinghast had been so abruptly broken. Ezra Weeden had frankly vowed vengeance; and though of a quiet and ordinarily mild disposition, was now gaining a hate-bred, dogged purpose which boded no good to the usurping husband.

On the seventh of May, 1765, Curwen's only child Ann was born; and was christened by the Rev. John Graves of King's Church, of which both husband and wife had become communicants shortly after their marriage, in order to compromise between their respective Congregational and Baptist affiliations. The record of this birth, as well as that of the marriage two years before, was stricken from most copies of the church and town annals where it ought to appear; and Charles Ward located both with the greatest difficulty after his discover of the widow's change of name had apprised him of his own relationship, and engendered the feverish interest which culminated in his madness. The birth entry, indeed, was found very curiously through correspondence with the heirs of the loyalist Dr. Graves, who had taken with him a duplicate set of records when he left his pastorate at the outbreak of the Revolution. Ward had tried this source because he knew that his great-great-grandmother Ann Tillinghast Potter had been an Episcopalian.

Shortly after the birth of his daughter, an event he seemed to welcome with a fervour greatly out of keeping with his usual coldness, Curwen resolved to sit for a portrait. This he had painted by a very gifted Scotsman named Cosmo Alexander, then a resident of Newport, and since famous as the early teacher of Gilbert Stuart. The likeness was said to have been executed on a wall-panel of the library of the house in Olney Court, but neither of the two old diaries mentioning it gave any hint of its ultimate disposition. At this period the erratic scholar shewed signs of unusual abstraction, and spent as much time as he possibly could at his farm on the Pawtuxet Road. He seemed, as was stated, in a condition of suppressed excitement or suspense; as if expecting some phenomenal thing or on the brink of some strange discovery. Chemistry or alchemy would appear to have played a great part, for he took from his house to the farm the greater number of his volumes on that subject.

His affectation of civic interest did not diminish, and he lost no opportunities for helping such leaders as Stephen Hopkins, Joseph Brown, and Benjamin West in their efforts to raise the cultural tone of the town, which was then much below the level of Newport in its patronage of the liberal arts. He had helped Daniel

Jenckes found his bookshop in 1763, and was thereafter his best customer; extending aid likewise to the struggling *Gazette* that appeared each Wednesday at the Sign of Shakespeare's Head. In politics he ardently supported Governor Hopkins against the Ward party whose prime strength was in Newport, and his really eloquent speech at Hacher's Hall in 1765 against the setting off of North Providence as a separate town with a pro-Ward vote in the General Assembly did more than any other thing to wear down the prejudice against him. But Ezra Weeden, who watched him closely, sneered cynically at all this outward activity; and freely swore it was no more than a mask for some nameless traffick with the blackest gulfs of Tartarus. The revengeful youth began a systematic study of the man and his doings whenever he was in port; spending hours at night by the wharves with a dory in readiness when he saw lights in the Curwen warehouses, and following the small boat which would sometimes steal quietly off and down the bay. He also kept as close a watch as possible on the Pawtuxet farm, and was once severely bitten by the dogs the old Indian couple loosed upon him.

2

In 1766 came the final change in Joseph Curwen. It was very sudden, and gained wide notice amongst the curious townsfolk; for the air of suspense and expectancy dropped like an old cloak, giving instant place to an ill-concealed exaltation of perfect triumph. Curwen seemed to have difficulty in restraining himself from public harangues on what he had found or learned or made; but apparently the need of secrecy was greater than the longing to share his rejoicing, for no explanation was ever offered by him. It was after this transition, which appears to have come early in July, that the sinister scholar began to astonish people by his possession of information which only their long-dead ancestors would seem to be able to impart.

But Curwen's feverish secret activities by no means ceased with this change. On the contrary, they tended rather to increase; so that more and more of his shipping business was handled by the captains whom he now bound to him by ties of fear as potent as those of bankruptcy had been. He altogether abandoned the slave trade, alleging that its profits were constantly decreasing. Every possible moment was spent at the Pawtuxet farm; although there were rumours now and then of his presence in places which, though not actually near graveyards, were yet so situated in relation to graveyards that thoughtful people wondered just how thorough the old merchant's change of habits really was. Ezra Weeden, though his periods of espionage were necessarily brief and intermittent on account of his sea voyaging, had a vindictive persistence which the bulk of the practical townsfolk and farmers lacked; and subjected Curwen's affairs to a scrutiny such as they had never had before.

Many of the odd manoeuvres of the strange merchant's vessels had been taken for granted on account of the unrest of the times, when every colonist seemed determined to resist the provisions of the Sugar Act which hampered a prominent traffick. Smuggling and evasion were the rule in Narragansett Bay, and nocturnal landings of illicit cargoes were continuous commonplaces. But Weeden, night after night following the lighters or small sloops which he saw steal off from the Curwen warehouses at the Town Street docks, soon felt assured that it was not merely His Majesty's armed ships which the sinister skulker was anxious to avoid. Prior to the change in 1766 these boats had for the most part contained chained negroes, who were carried down and across the bay and landed at an obscure point on the shore just north of Pawtuxet; being afterward driven up the bluff and across country to the Curwen farm, where they were locked in that enormous stone outbuilding which had only five high narrow slits for windows. After that change, however, the whole programme was altered. Importation of slaves ceased at once, and for a time Curwen abandoned his midnight sailings. Then, about the spring of 1767, a new policy appeared. Once more the lighters grew wont to put out from the black, silent docks, and this time they would go down the bay some distance, perhaps as far as Namquit Point, where they would meet and receive cargo from strange ships of considerable size and widely varied appearance. Curwen's sailors would then deposit this cargo at the usual point on the shore, and transport it overland to the farm; locking it in the same cryptical stone building which had formerly received the negroes. The cargo consisted almost wholly of boxes and cases, of which a large proportion were oblong and heavy and disturbingly suggestive of coffins.

Weeden always watched the farm with unremitting assiduity; visiting it each night for long periods, and seldom letting a week go by without a sight except when the ground bore a footprint-revealing snow. Even then he would often walk as close as possible in the travelled road or on the ice of the neighbouring river to see what tracks others might have left. Finding his own vigils interrupted by nautical duties, he hired a tavern companion named Eleazar Smith to continue the survey during his absence; and between them the two could have set in motion some extraordinary rumours. That they did not do so was only because they knew the effect of publicity would be to warn their quarry and make further progress impossible. Instead, they wished to learn something definite before taking any action. What they did learn must have been startling indeed, and Charles Ward spoke many times to his parents of his regret at Weeden's later burning of his notebooks. All that can be told of their discoveries is what Eleazar Smith jotted down in a non too coherent diary, and what other diarists and letter-writers have timidly repeated from the statements which they finally made – and according to which the farm was only the outer shell of some vast and revolting menace, of a scope and depth too profound and intangible for more than shadowy comprehension.

It is gathered that Weeden and Smith became early convinced that a great series of tunnels and catacombs, inhabited by a very sizeable staff of persons besides the old Indian and his wife, underlay the farm. The house was an old peaked relic of the middle seventeenth century with enormous stack chimney and diamond-paned lattice windows, the laboratory being in a lean-to toward the north, where the roof came nearly to the ground. This building stood clear of any other; yet judging by the different voices heard at odd times within, it must have been accessible through secret passages beneath. These voices, before 1766, were mere mumblings and negro whisperings and frenzied screams, coupled with curious chants or invocations. After that date, however, they assumed a very singular and terrible cast as they ran the gamut betwixt dronings of dull acquiescence and explosions of frantic pain or fury, rumblings of conversations and whines of entreaty, pantings of eagerness and shouts of protest. They appeared to be in different languages, all known to Curwen, whose rasping accents were frequently distinguishable in reply, reproof, or threatening.

Sometimes it seemed that several persons must be in the house; Curwen, certain captives, and the guards of those captives. There were voices of a sort that neither Weeden nor Smith had ever heard before despite their wide knowledge of foreign parts, and many that they did seem to place as belonging to this or that nationality. The nature of the conversations seemed always a kind of catechism, as if Curwen were extorting some sort of information from terrified or rebellious prisoners.

Weeden had many verbatim reports of overheard scraps in his notebook, for English, French, and Spanish, which he knew, were frequently used; but of these nothing has survived. He did, however, say that besides a few ghoulish dialogues in which the past affairs of Providence families were concerned, most of the questions and answers he could understand were historical or scientific; occasionally pertaining to very remote places and ages. Once, for example, an alternately raging and sullen figure was questioned in French about the Black Prince's massacre at Limoges in 1370, as if there were some hidden reason which he ought to know. Curwen asked the prisoner – if prisoner he were – whether the order to slay was given because of the Sign of the Goat found on the altar in the ancient Roman crypt beneath the Cathedral, or whether the Dark Man of the Haute Vienne had spoken the Three Words. Failing to obtain replies, the inquisitor had seemingly resorted to extreme means; for there was a terrific shriek followed by silence and muttering and a bumping sound.

None of these colloquies was ever ocularly witnessed, since the windows were always heavily draped. Once, though, during a discourse in an unknown tongue, a shadow was seen on the curtain which startled Weeden exceedingly; reminding him of one of the puppets in a show he had seen in the autumn of 1764 in Hacher's Hall, when a man from Germantown, Pennsylvania, had given a clever mechanical spectacle advertised as

"A View of the Famous City of Jerusalem, in which are represented Jerusalem, the Temple of Solomon, his Royal Throne, the noted Towers, and Hills, likewise the Suffering of Our Saviour from the Garden of Gethsemane to the Cross on the Hill of Golgotha; an artful piece of Statuary, Worthy to be seen by the Curious."

It was on this occasion that the listener, who had crept close to the window of the front room whence the speaking proceeded, gave a start which roused the old Indian pair and caused them to loose the dogs on him. After that no more conversations were ever heard in the house, and Weeden and Smith concluded that Curwen had transferred his field of action to regions below.

That such regions in truth existed, seemed amply clear from many things. Faint cries and groans unmistakably came up now and then from what appeared to be the solid earth in places far from any structure; whilst hidden in the bushes along the river-bank in the rear, where the high ground sloped steeply down to the valley of the Pawtuxet, there was found an arched oaken door in a frame of heavy masonry, which was obviously an entrance to caverns within the hill. When or how these catacombs could have been constructed, Weeden was unable to say; but he frequently pointed out how easily the place might have been reached by bands of unseen workmen from the river. Joseph Curwen put his mongrel seamen to diverse uses indeed! During the heavy spring rains of 1769 the two watchers kept a sharp eye on the steep river-bank to see if any subterrene secrets might be washed to light, and were rewarded by the sight of a profusion of both human and animal bones in places where deep gullies had been worn in the banks. Naturally there might be many explanations of such things in the rear of a stock farm, and a locality where old Indian bury-grounds were common, but Weeden and Smith drew their own inferences.

It was in January 1770, whilst Weeden and Smith were still debating vainly on what, if anything, to think or do about the whole bewildering business, that the incident of the *Fortaleza* occurred. Exasperated by the burning of the revenue sloop *Liberty* at Newport during the previous summer, the customs fleet under Admiral Wallace had adopted an increased vigilance concerning strange vessels; and on this occasion His Majesty's armed schooner *Cygnet*, under Capt. Charles Leslie, captured after a short pursuit one early morning the scow *Fortaleza* of Barcelona, Spain, under Capt. Manuel Arruda, bound according to its log from Grand Cairo, Egypt, to Providence. When searched for contraband material, this ship revealed the astonishing fact that its cargo consisted exclusively of Egyptian mummies, consigned to "Sailor A. B. C.", who would come to remove his goods in a lighter just off Namquit Point and whose identity Capt. Arruda felt himself in honour bound not to reveal. The Vice-Admiralty at Newport, at a loss what to do in view of the non-contraband nature of the cargo on the one hand and of the unlawful secrecy of the entry on the other hand, compromised on Collector Robinson's recommendation by freeing the ship but forbidding it a port in Rhode Island waters. There were later rumours of its having been seen in Boston Harbour, though it never openly entered the Port of Boston.

This extraordinary incident did not fail of wide remark in Providence, and there were not many who doubted the existence of some connexion between the cargo of mummies and the sinister Joseph Curwen. His exotic studies and his curious chemical importations being common knowledge, and his fondness for graveyards being common suspicion; it did not take much imagination to link him with a freakish importation which could not conceivably have been destined for anyone else in the town. As if conscious of this natural belief, Curwen took care to speak casually on several occasions of the chemical value of the balsams found in mummies; thinking perhaps that he might make the affair seem less unnatural, yet stopping just short of admitting his participation. Weeden and Smith, of course, felt no doubt whatsoever of the significance of the thing; and indulged in the wildest theories concerning Curwen and his monstrous labours.

The following spring, like that of the year before, had heavy rains; and the watchers kept careful track of teh river-bank behind the Curwen farm. Large sections were washed away, and a certain number of bones discovered; but no glimpse was afforded of any actual subterranean chambers or burrows. Something was rumoured, however, at the village of Pawtuxet about a mile below, where the river flows in falls over a rocky terrace to join the placed landlocked cove. There, where quaint old cottages climbed the hill from the rustic bridge, and fishing-smacks lay anchored at their sleepy docks, a vague report went round of things that were floating down the river and flashing into sight for a minute as they went over the falls. Of course the Pawtuxet in a long river which winds through many settled regions abounding in graveyards, and of course the spring rains had been very heavy; but the fisherfolk about the bridge did not like the wild way that one of the things stared as it shot down to the still waters below, or the way that another half cried out although its condition had greatly departed from that of objects which normally cried out. That rumour sent Smith – for Weeden was just then at sea – in haste to the river-bank behind the farm; where surely enough there remained the evidence of an extensive cave-in. There was, however, no trace of a passage into the steep bank; for the miniature avalanche had left behind a solid wall of mixed earth and shrubbery from aloft. Smith went to the extent of some experimental digging, but was deterred by lack of success – or perhaps by fear of possible success. It is interesting to speculate on what the persistent and revengeful Weeden would have done had he been ashore at the time.

3

By the autumn of 1770 Weeden decided that the time was ripe to tell others of his discoveries; for he had a large number of facts to link together, and a second eye-witness to refute the possible charge that jealousy and vindictiveness had spurred his fancy. As his first confidant he selected Capt. James Mathewson of the *Enterprise*, who on the one hand knew him well enough not to doubt his veracity, and on the other hand was sufficiently influential in the town to be heard in turn with respect. The colloquy took place in an upper room of Sabin's Tavern near the docks, with Smith present to corroborate virtually every statement; and it could be seen that Capt. Mathewson was tremendously impressed. Like nearly everyone else in the town, he had had black suspicions of his own anent Joseph Curwen; hence it needed only this confirmation and enlargement of data to convince him absolutely. At the end of the conference he was very grave, and enjoined strict silence upon the two younger men. He would, he said, transmit the information separately to some ten or son of the most learned and prominent citizens of Providence; ascertaining their views and following whatever advice they might have to offer. Secrecy would probably be essential in any case, for this was no matter that the town constables or militia could cope with; and above all else the excitable

42

crowd must be kept in ignorance, lest there be enacted in these already troublous times a repetition of that frightful Salem panic of less than a century before which had first brought Curwen hither.

The right persons to tell, he believed, would be Dr. Benjamin West, whose pamphlet on the late transit of Venus proved him a scholar and keen thinker; Rev. James Manning, President of the College which had just moved up from Warren and was temporarily housed in the new King Street schoolhouse awaiting the completion of its building on the hill above Presbyterian-Lane; ex-Governor Stephen Hopkins, who had been a member of the Philosophical Society at Newport, and was a man of very broad perceptions; John Carter, publisher of the *Gazette*; all four of the Brown brothers, John, Joseph, Nicholas, and Moses, who formed the recognised local magnates, and of whom Joseph was an amateur scientist of parts; old Dr. Jabez Bowen, whose erudition was considerable, and who had much first-hand knowledge of Curwen's odd purchases; and Capt. Abraham Whipple, a privateersman of phenomenal boldness and energy who could be counted on to lead in any active measures needed. These men, if favourable, might eventually be brought together for collective deliberation; and with them would rest the responsibility of deciding whether or not to inform the Governor of the Colony, Joseph Wanton of Newport, before taking action.

The mission of Capt. Mathewson prospered beyond his highest expectations; for whilst he found one or two of the chosen confidants somewhat sceptical of the possible ghastly side of Weeden's tale, there was not one who did not think it necessary to take some sort of secret and coördinated action. Curwen, it was clear, formed a vague potential menace to the welfare of the town and Colony; and must be eliminated at any cost. Late in December

1770 a group of eminent townsmen met at the home of Stephen Hopkins and debated tentative measures. Weeden's notes, which he had given to Capt. Mathewson, were carefully read; and he and Smith were summoned to give testimony anent details. Something very like fear seized the whole assemblage before the meeting was over, though there ran through that fear a grim determination which Capt. Whipple's bluff and resonant profanity best expressed. They would not notify the Governor, because a more than legal course seemed necessary. With hidden powers of uncertain extent apparently at his disposal, Curwen was not a man who could safely be warned to leave town. Nameless reprisals might ensue, and even if the sinister creature complied, the removal would be no more than the shifting of an unclean burden to another place. The times were lawless, and men who had flouted the King's revenue forces for years were not the ones to balk at sterner things when duty impelled. Curwen must be surprised at his Pawtuxet farm by a large raiding-party of seasoned privateersmen and given one decisive chance to explain himself. If he proved a madman, amusing himself with shrieks and imaginary conversations in different voices, he would be properly confined. If something graver appeared, and if the underground horrors indeed turned out to be real, he and all with him must die. It could be done quietly, and even the widow and her father need not be told how it came about.

While these serious steps were under discussion there occurred in the town an incident so terrible and inexplicable that for a time little else was mentioned for miles around. In the middle of a moon-light January night with heavy snow underfoot there resounded over the river and up the hill a shocking series of cries which brought sleepy heads to every window; and people around Weybosset Point saw a great white thing plunging frantically along the badly cleared space in front of the Turk's Head. There was a baying of dogs in the distance, but this subsided as soon as the clamour of the awakened town became audible. Parties of men with lanterns and muskets hurried out to see what was happening, but nothing rewarded their search. The next morning, however, a giant, muscular body, stark naked, was found on the jams of ice around the southern piers of the Great Bridge, where the Long Dock stretched out beside Abbott's distil-house, and the identity of this object became a theme for endless speculation and whispering. It was not so much the younger as the older folk who whispered, for only in the patriarchs did that rigid face with horror-bulging eyes strike any chord of memory. They, shaking as they did so, exchanged furtive murmurs of wonder and fear; for in those stiff, hideous features lay a resemblance so marvellous as to be almost an identity – and that identity was with a man who had died full fifty years before.

Ezra Weeden was present at the finding; and remembering the baying of the night before, set out along Weybosset Street and across Muddy Dock Bridge whence the sound had come. He had a curious expectancy, and was not surprised when, reaching the edge of the settled district where the street merged into the Pawtuxet Road, he came upon some very curious tracks in the snow. The naked giant had been pursued by dogs and many booted men, and the returning tracks of the hounds and their masters could be easily traced. They had given up the chase upon coming too near the town. Weeden smiled grimly, and as a perfunctory detail traced the footprints back to their source. It was the Pawtuxet farm of Joseph Curwen, as he well knew it would be; and he would have given much had the yard been less confusingly trampled. As it was, he dared not seem too interested in full daylight. Dr. Bowen, to whom

Weeden went at once with his report, performed an autopsy on the strange corpse, and discovered peculiarities which baffled him utterly. The digestive tracts of the huge man seemed never to have been in use, whilst the whole skin had a coarse, loosely knit texture impossible to account for. Impressed by what the old men whispered of this body's likeness to the long-dead blacksmith Daniel Green, whose great-grandson Aaron Hoppin was a supercargo in Curwen's employ, Weeden asked casual questions till he found where Green was buried. That night a party of ten visited the old North Burying Ground opposite Herrenden's Lane and opened a grave. They found it vacant, precisely as they had expected.

Meanwhile arrangements had been made with the post riders to intercept Joseph Curwen's mail, and shortly before the incident of the naked body there was found a letter from one Jedediah Orne of Salem which made the coöperating citizens think deeply. Parts of it, copied and preserved in the private archives of the Smith family where Charles Ward found it, ran as follows.

"I delight that you continue in ye Gett'g at Olde Matters in your Way, and doe not think better was done at Mr. Hutchinson's in Salem-Village. Certainely, there was Noth'g but ye liveliest Awfulness in that which H. rais'd upp from What he cou'd gather onlie a part of. What you sente, did not Worke, whether because of Any Thing miss'g, or because ye Wordes were not Righte from my Speak'g or yr Copy'g. I alone am at a Loss. I have not ye Chymicall art to followe Borellus, and owne my Self confounded by ye VII. Booke of ye *Necronomicon* that you recommende. But I wou'd have you Observe what was told to us aboute tak'g Care whom to calle upp, for you are Sensible what Mr. Mather writ in ye Magnalia of ———, and can judge how truely that Horrendous thing is reported. I say to you againe, doe not call up Any that you can not put downe; by the Which I meane, Any that can in Turne call up Somewhat against you, whereby your Powerfullest Devices may not be of use. Ask of the Lesser, lest the Greater shal not wish to Answer, and shal commande more than you. I was frighted when I read of your know'g what Ben Zariatnatmik hadde in his ebony Boxe, for I was conscious who must have tolde you. And againe I ask that you shalle write me as Jedediah and not Simon. In this Community a Man may not live too long, and you knowe my Plan by which I came back as my Son. I am desirous you will Acquaint me with what ye Black Man learnt from Sylvanus Cocidius in ye Vault, under ye Roman Wall, and will be oblig'd for ye lend'g of ye MS. you speak of.

Another and unsigned letter from Philadelphia provoked equal thought, especially for the following passage:

"I will observe what you say respecting the sending of Accounts only by yr Vessels, but can not always be certain when to expect them. In the Matter spoke of, I require onlie one more thing; but wish to be sure I apprehend you exactly. You inform me, that no Part must be missing if the finest Effects are to be had, but you can not but know how hard it is to be sure. It seems a great Hazard and Burthen to take away the whole Box, and in Town (i.e. St. Peter's, St. Paul's, St. Mary's or Christ Church) it can scarce be done at all. But I know what Imperfections were in the one I rais'd up October last, and how many live Specimens you were forc'd to imploy before you hit upon the right Mode in the year 1766; so will be guided by you in all Matters. I am impatient for yr Brig, and inquire daily at Mr. Biddle's Wharf."

A third suspicious letter was in an unknown tongue and even an unknown alphabet. In the Smith diary found by Charles Ward a single oft-repeated combination of characters is clumsily copied; and authorities at Brown University have pronounced the alphabet Amharic or Abyssinian, although they do not recognise the word. None of these epistles was ever delivered to Curwen, though the disappearance of Jedediah Orne from Salem as recorded shortly afterward shewed that the Providence men took certain quiet steps. The Pennsylvania Historical Society also has some curious letters received by Dr. Shippen regarding the presence of an unwholesome character in Philadelphia. But more decisive steps were in the air, and it is in the secret assemblages of sworn and tested sailors and faithful old privateersmen in the Brown warehouses by night that we must look for the main fruits of Weeden's disclosures. Slowly and surely a plan of campaign was under development which would leave no trace of Joseph Curwen's noxious mysteries.

Curwen, despite all precautions, apparently felt that something was in the wind; for he was now remarked to wear an unusually worried look. His coach was seen at all hours in the town and on the Pawtuxet Road, and he dropped little by little the air of forced geniality with which he had latterly sought to combat the town's prejudice. The nearest neighbours to his farm, the Fenners, one night remarked a great shaft of light shooting into the sky from some aperture in the roof of that cryptical stone building with the high, excessively narrow windows; an event which they quickly communicated to John Brown in Providence. Mr. Brown had become the executive leader of the select group bent on Curwen's extirpation, and had informed the Fenners that some action was about to be taken. This he deemed needful because of the impossibility of their not witnessing the final raid; and he explained his course by saying that Curwen was known to be a spy of the customs officers at Newport, against whom the hand of every Providence skipper, merchant, and farmer was openly or clandestinely raised. Whether the ruse was wholly believed by neighbours who had seen so many queer things is not certain; but at any rate the Fenners were willing to connect any evil with a man of such queer ways. To them Mr. Brown had entrusted the duty of watching the Curwen farmhouse, and of regularly reporting every incident which took place there.

4

The probability that Curwen was on guard and attempting unusual things, as suggested by the odd shaft of light, precipitated at last the action so carefully devised by the band of serious citizens. According to the Smith diary a company of about 100 men met at 10 p.m. on Friday, April 12th, 1771, in the great room of Thurston's Tavern at the Sign of the Golden Lion on Weybosset Point across the Bridge. Of the guiding group of prominent men in addition to the leader John Brown there were present Dr. Bowen, with his case of surgical instruments, President Manning without the great periwig (the largest in the Colonies) for which he was noted, Governor Hopkins, wrapped in his dark cloak and accompanied by his seafaring brother Esek, whom he had initiated at the last moment with the permission of the rest, John Carter, Capt. Mathewson, and Capt. Whipple, who was to lead the actual raiding party. These chiefs conferred apart in a rear chamber, after which Capt. Whipple emerged to the great room and gave the gathered seamen their last oaths and instructions. Eleazar Smith was with the leaders as they sat in the rear apartment awaiting the arrival of Ezra Weeden, whose duty was to keep track of Curwen and report the departure of his coach for the farm.

About 10:30 a heavy rumble was heard on the Great Bridge, followed by the sound of a coach in the street outside; and at that hour there was no need of waiting for Weeden in order to know that the doomed man had set out for his last night of unhallowed wizardry. A moment later, as the receding coach clattered faintly over the Muddy Dock Bridge, Weeden appeared; and the raiders fell silently into military order in the street, shouldering the firelocks, fowling-pieces, or whaling harpoons which they had with them. Weeden and Smith were with the party, and of the deliberating citizens there were present for active service Capt. Whipple, the leader, Capt. Esek Hopkins, John Carter, President Manning, Capt. Mathewson, and Dr. Bowen; together with Moses Brown, who had come up at the eleventh hour though absent from the preliminary session in the tavern. All these freemen and their hundred sailors began the long march without delay, grim and a trifle apprehensive as they left the Muddy Dock behind and mounted the gentle rise of Broad Street toward the Pawtuxet Road. Just beyond Elder Snow's church some of the men turned back to take a parting look at Providence lying outspread under the early spring stars. Steeples and gables rose dark and shapely, and salt breezes swept up gently from the cove north of the Bridge. Vega was climbing above the great hill across the water, whose crest of trees was broken by the roof-line of the unfinished College edifice. At the foot of that hill, and along the narrow mounting lanes of its side, the old town dreamed; Old Providence, for whose safety and sanity so monstrous and colossal a blasphemy was about to be wiped out.

An hour and a quarter later the raiders arrived, as previously agreed, at the Fenner farmhouse; where they heard a final report on their intended victim. He had reached his farm over half an hour before, and the strange light had soon afterward shot once more into the sky, but there were no lights in any visible windows. This was always the case of late. Even as this news was given another great glare arose toward the south, and the party realised that they had indeed come close to the scene of awesome and unnatural wonders. Capt. Whipple now ordered his force to separate into three divisions; one of twenty men under Eleazar Smith to strike across to the shore and guard the landing-place against possible reinforcements for Curwen until summoned by a messenger for desperate service, a second of twenty men under Capt. Esek Hopkins to steal down into the river valley behind the Curwen farm and demolish with axes or gunpowder the oaken door in the high, steep bank, and the third to close in on the house and adjacent buildings themselves. Of this division one third was to be led by Capt. Mathewson to the cryptical stone edifice with high narrow windows, another third to follow Capt. Whipple himself to the main farmhouse, and the remaining third to preserve a circle around the whole group of buildings until summoned by a final emergency signal.

The river party would break down the hillside door at the sound of a single whistle-blast, then wait and capture anything which might issue from the regions within. At the sound of two whistle-blasts it would advance through the aperture to oppose the enemy or join the rest of the raiding contingent. The party at the stone building would accept these respective signals in an analogous manner; forcing an entrance at the first, and at the second descending whatever passage into the ground might be discovered, and joining the general or focal warfare expected to take place within the caverns. A third or emergency signal of three blasts would summon the immediate reserve from its general guard duty; its twenty men dividing equally and entering the unknown depths through both farmhouse and stone building. Capt. Whipple's belief in the existence of catacombs was absolute, and he took no alternative into consideration when making his plans. He had with him a whistle of great power and shrillness, and did not fear any upsetting or misunderstanding of signals. The final reserve at the landing, of course, was nearly out of the whistle's range; hence would require a special messenger if needed for help. Moses Brown and John Carter went with Capt. Hopkins to the river-bank, while President Manning was detailed with Capt. Mathewson to the stone building. Dr. Bowen, with Ezra Weeden, remained in Capt. Whipple's party which was to storm the farmhouse itself. The attack was to begin as soon as a messenger from Capt. Hopkins had joined Capt. Whipple to notify him of the river party's readiness. The leader would then deliver the loud single blast, and the various advance parties would commence their simultaneous attack on three points. Shortly before 1 a.m. the three divisions left the Fenner farmhouse; one to guard the landing, another to seek the river valley and the hillside door, and the third to subdivide and attend to teh actual buildings of the Curwen farm.

Eleazar Smith, who accompanied the shore-guarding party, records in his diary an uneventful march and a long wait on the bluff by the bay; broken once by what seemed to be the distant sound of the signal whistle and again by a peculiar muffled blend of roaring and crying and a powder blast which seemed to come from the same direction. Later on one man thought he caught some distant gunshots, and still later Smith himself felt the throb of titanic and thunderous words resounding in upper air. It was just before dawn that a single haggard messenger with wild eyes and a hideous unknown odour about his clothing appeared and told the detachment to disperse quietly to their homes and never again think or speak of the night's doings or of him who had been Joseph Curwen. Something about the bearing of the messenger carried a conviction which his mere words could never have conveyed; for though he was a seaman well known to many of them, there was something obscurely lost or gained in his soul which set him for evermore apart. It was the same later on when they met other old companions who had gone into that zone of horror. Most of them had lost or gained something imponderable and indescribable. They had seen or heard or felt something which was not for human creatures, and could not forget it. From them there was never any gossip, for to even the commonest of mortal instincts there are terrible boundaries. And from that single messenger the party at the shore caught a nameless awe which almost sealed their own lips. Very few are the rumours which ever came from any of them, and Eleazar Smith's diary is the only written record which has survived from that whole expedition which set forth from the Sign of the Golden Lion under the stars.

Charles Ward, however, discovered another vague sidelight in some Fenner correspondence which he found in New London, where he knew another branch of the family had lived. It seems that the Fenners, from whose house the doomed farm was distantly visible, had watched the departing columns of raiders; and had heard very clearly the angry barking of the Curwen dogs, followed by the first shrill blast which precipitated the attack. This blast had been followed by a repetition of the great shaft of light from the stone building, and in another moment, after a quick sounding of the second signal ordering a general invasion, there had come a subdued prattle of musketry followed by a horrible roaring cry which the correspondent Luke Fenner had represented in his epistle by the characters 'Waaaahrrrrr-R'waaahrrr.'

This cry, however, had possessed a quality which no mere writing could convey, and the correspondent mentions that his mother fainted completely at the sound. It was later repeated less loudly, and further but more muffled evidences of gunfire ensued; together with a loud explosion of powder from the direction of the river. About an hour afterward all the dogs began to bark frightfully, and there were vague ground rumblings so marked that the candlesticks tottered on the mantelpiece. A strong smell of sulphur was noted; and Luke Fenner's father declared that he heard the third or emergency whistle signal, though the others failed to detect it. Muffled musketry sounded again, followed by a deep scream less piercing but even more horrible than the those which had preceded it; a kind of throaty, nastily plastic cough or gurgle whose quality as a scream must have come more from its continuity and psychological import than from its actual acoustic value.

Then the flaming thing burst into sight at a point where the Curwen farm ought to lie, and the human cries of desperate and frightened men were heard. Muskets flashed and cracked, and the flaming thing fell to the ground. S second flaming thing appeared, and a shriek of human origin was plainly distinguished. Fenner wrote that he could even gather a few words belched in frenzy: Almighty, protect thy lamb! Then there were more shots, and the second flaming thing fell. After that came silence for about three-quarters of an hour; at the end of which time little Arthur Fenner, Luke's brother, exclaimed that he saw "a red fog" going up to the stars from the accursed farm in the distance. No one but the child

54

can testify to this, but Luke admits the significant coincidence implied by the panic of almost convulsive fright which at the same moment arched the backs and stiffened the fur of the three cats then within the room.

Five minutes later a chill wind blew up, and the air became suffused with an intolerable stench that only the strong freshness of the sea could have prevented its being notice by the shore party or by any wakeful souls in the Pawtuxet village. This stench was nothing which any of the Fenners had ever encountered before, and produced a kind of clutching, amorphous fear beyond that of the tomb or the charnel-house. Close upon it came the awful voice which no hapless hearer will ever be able to forget. It thundered out of the sky like a doom, and windows rattled as its echoes died away. It was deep and musical; powerful as a bass organ, but evil as the forbidden books of the Arabs. What it said no man can tell, for it spoke in an unknown tongue, but this is the writing Luke Fenner set down to portray the daemoniac intonations: 'DEESMEES JESHET BONE DOSEFE DUVEMA ENITEMOSS.' Not till the year 1919 did any soul link this crude transcript with anything else in mortal knowledge, but Charles Ward paled as he recognised what Mirandola had denounced in shudders as the ultimate horror among black magic's incantations.

An unmistakable human shout or deep chorused scream seemed to answer this malign wonder from the Curwen farm, after which the unknown stench grew complex with an added odour equally intolerable. A wailing distinctly different from the scream now burst out, and was protracted ululantly in rising and falling paroxysms. At times it became almost articulate, though no auditor could trace any definite words; and at one point it seemed to verge toward the confines of diabolic and hysterical laughter. Then a yell of utter, ultimate fright and stark madness wrenched from scores of human throats – a yell which came strong and clear despite the depth from which it must have burst; after which darkness and silence ruled all things. Spirals of acrid smoke ascended to blot out the stars, though no flames appeared and no buildings were observed to be gone or injured on the following day.

Toward dawn two frightened messengers with monstrous and unplaceable odours saturating their clothing knocked at the Fenner door and requested a keg of rum, for which they paid very well indeed. One of them told the family that the affair of Joseph Curwen was over, and that the events of the night were not to be mentioned again. Arrogant as the order seemed, the aspect of him who gave it took away all resentment and lent it a fearsome authority; so that only these furtive letters of Luke Fenner, which he urged his Connecticut relative to destroy, remain to tell what was seen and heard. The non-compliance of that relative, whereby the letters were saved after all, has alone kept the matter from a merciful oblivion. Charles Ward had one detail to add as a result of a long canvass of Pawtuxet residents for ancestral traditions. Old Charles Slocum of that village said that there was known to his grandfather a queer rumour concerning a charred, distorted body found in the fields a week after the death of Joseph Curwen was announced. What kept the talk alive was the notion that this body, so far as could be seen in its burnt and twisted condition, was neither thoroughly human nor wholly allied to any animal which Pawtuxet folk had ever seen or read about.

Not one man who participated in that terrible raid could ever be induced to say a word concerning it, and every fragment of the vague data which survives comes from those outside the final fighting party. There is something frightful in the care with which these actual raiders destroyed each scrap which bore the least allusion to the matter. Eight sailors had been killed, but although their bodies were not produced their families were satisfied with the statement that a clash with customs officers had occurred. The same statement also covered the numerous cases of wounds, all of which were extensively bandaged and treated only by Dr. Jabez Bowen, who had accompanied the party. Hardest to explain was the nameless odour clinging to all the raiders, a thing which was discussed for weeks. Of the citizen leaders, Capt. Whipple and Moses Brown were most severely hurt, and letters of their wives testify the bewilderment which their reticence and close guarding of their bandages produced. Psychologically every participant was aged, sobered, and shaken. It is fortunate that they were all strong men of action and simple, orthodox religionists, for with more subtle introspectiveness and mental complexity they would have fared ill indeed. President Manning was the most disturbed; but even he outgrew the darkest shadow, and smothered memories in prayers. Every man of those leaders had a stirring part to play in later years, and it is perhaps fortunate that this is so. Little more than a twelvemonth afterward Capt. Whipple led the mob who burnt the revenue ship *Gaspee*, and in this bold act we may trace one step in the blotting out of unwholesome images.

There was delivered to the widow of Joseph Curwen a sealed leaden coffin of curious design, obviously found ready on the spot when needed, in which she was told he husband's body lay. He had, it was explained, been killed in a customs battle about which it was not politic to give details. More than this no tongue ever uttered of Joseph Curwen's end, and Charles Ward had only a single hint wherewith to construct a theory. This hint was the merest thread – a shaky underscoring of a passage in Jedediah Orne's confiscated letter to Curwen, as partly copied in Ezra Weeden's handwriting. The copy was found in the possession of Smith's descendants; and we are left to decide whether Weeden gave it to his companion after the end, as a mute clue to the abnormality which had occurred, or whether, as is more probable, Smith had it before, and added the underscoring himself from what he had managed to extract from his friend by shrewd guessing and adroit cross-questioning. The underlined passage is merely this:

I say to you againe, doe not call up Any that you can not put downe; by the Which I meane, Any that can in Turne call up Somewhat against you, whereby your Powerfullest Devices may not be of use. Ask of the Lesser, lest the Greater shal not wish to Answer, and shal commande more than you.

In the light of this passage, and reflecting on what last unmentionable allies a beaten man might try to summon in his direst extremity, Charles Ward may well have wondered whether any citizen of Providence killed Joseph Curwen.

The deliberate effacement of every memory of the dead man from Providence life and annals was vastly aided by the influence of the raiding leaders. They had not at first meant to be so thorough, and had allowed the widow and her father and child to remain in ignorance of the true conditions; but Capt. Tillinghast was an astute man, and soon uncovered enough rumours to whet his horror and cause him to demand that he daughter and granddaughter change their name, burn the library and all remaining papers, and chisel the inscription from the slate slab above Joseph Curwen's grave. He knew Capt. Whipple well, and probably extracted more hints from that bluff mariner and anyone else ever gained repecting the end of the accursed sorcerer.

From that time on the obliteration of Curwen's memory became increasingly rigid, extending at last by common consent even to the town records and files of the *Gazette*. It can be compared in spirit only to the hush that lay on Oscar Wilde's name for a decade after his disgrace, and in extent only to the fate of that sinful King of Runazar in Lord Dunsany's tale, whom the Gods decided must not only cease to be, but must cease ever to have been.

Mrs. Tillinghast, as the widow became known after 1772, sold the house in Olney Court and resided with her father in Power's Lane till her death in 1817. The farm at Pawtuxet, shunned by every living soul, remained to moulder through the years; and seemed to decay with unaccountable rapidity. By 1780 only the stone and brickwork were standing, and by 1800 even these had fallen to shapeless heaps. None ventured to pierce the tangled shrubbery on the river-bank behind which the hillside door may have lain, nor did any try to frame a definite image of the scenes amidst which Joseph Curwen departed from the horrors he had wrought.

Only robust old Capt. Whipple was heard by alert listeners to mutter once in a while to himself, "Pox on that ———, but he had no business to laugh while he screamed. 'Twas as though the damn'd ——— had some'at up his sleeve. For half a crown I'd burn his ——— home."

CHAPTER THREE

A Search and an Evocation

1

Charles Ward, as we have seen, first learned in 1918 of his descent from Joseph Curwen. That he at once took an intense interest in everything pertaining to the bygone mystery is not to be wondered at; for every vague rumour that he had heard of Curwen now became something vital to himself, in whom flowed Curwen's blood. No spirited and imaginative genealogist could have done otherwise than begin forthwith an avid and systematic collection of Curwen data.

In his first delvings there was not the slightest attempt at secrecy; so that even Dr. Lyman hesitates to date the youth's madness from any period before the close of 1919. He talked freely with his family – though his mother was not particularly pleased to own an ancestor like Curwen – and with the officials of the various museums and libraries he visited. In applying to private families for records thought to be in their possession he made no concealment of his object, and shared the somewhat amused scepticism with which the accounts of the old diarists and letter-writers were regarded. He often expressed a keen wonder as to what really had taken place a century and a half before at the Pawtuxet farmhouse whose site he vainly tried to find, and what Joseph Curwen really had been.

When he came across the Smith diary and archives and encountered the letter from Jedediah Orne he decided to visit Salem and look up Curwen's early activities and connexions there, which he did during the Easter vacation of 1919. At the Essex Institute, which was well known to him from former sojourns in the glamorous old town of crumbling Puritan gables and clustered gambrel roofs, he was very kindly received, and unearthed there a considerable amount of Curwen data. He found that his ancestor was born in Salem-Village, now Danvers, seven miles from town, on the eighteenth of February (O.S.) 1662-3; and that he had run away to sea at the age of fifteen, not appearing again for nine years, when he returned with the speech, dress, and manners of a native Englishman and settled in Salem proper. At that time he had little to do with his family, but spent most of his hours with the curious books he had brought from Europe, and the strange chemicals which came for him on ships from England, France, and Holland. Certain trips of his into the country were the objects of much local inquisitiveness, and were whisperingly associated with vague rumours of fires on the hills at night.

Curwen's only close friends had been one Edward Hutchinson of Salem-Village and one Simon Orne of Salem. With these men he was often seen in conference about the Common, and visits among them were by no means infrequent. Hutchinson had a house well out toward the woods, and it was not altogether liked by sensitive people because of the sounds heard there at night. He was said to entertain strange visitors, and the lights seen from his windows were not always of the same colour. The knowledge he displayed concerning long-dead persons and long-forgotten events was considered distinctly unwholesome, and he disappeared about the time the witchcraft panic began, never to be heard from again. At that time Joseph Curwen also departed, but his settlement in Providence was soon learned of. Simon Orne lived in Salem until 1720, when his failure to grow visibly old began to excite attention. He thereafter disappeared, though thirty years later his precise counterpart and self-styled son turned up to claim his property. The claim was allowed on the strength of documents in Simon Orne's known hand, and Jedediah Orne continued to dwell in Salem till 1771, when certain letters from Providence citizens to the Rev. Thomas Barnard and others brought about his quiet removal to parts unknown.

Certain documents by and about all of the strange characters were available at teh Essex Institute, the Court House, and the Registry of Deeds, and included both harmless commonplaces such as land titles and bills of sale, and furtive fragments of a more provocative nature. There were four or five unmistakable allusions to them on the witchcraft trial records; as when one Hepzibah Lawson swore on July 10, 1692, at the Court of Oyer and Terminer under Judge Hathorne, that: 'fortie Witches and the Blacke Man were wont to meete in the Woodes behind Mr. Hutchinson's house', and one Amity How declared at a session of August 8th before Judge Gedney that:'Mr. G. B. (Rev. George Burroughs) on that Nighte putt ye Divell his Marke upon Bridget S., Jonathan A., *Simon O.,* Deliverance W., *Joseph C.*, Susan P., Mehitable C., and Deborah B.'

Then there was a catalogue of Hutchinson's uncanny library as found after his disappearance, and an unfinished manuscript in his handwriting, couched in a cipher none could read. Ward had a photostatic copy of this manuscript made, and began to work casually on the cipher as soon as it was delivered to him. After the following August his labours on the cipher became intense and feverish, and there is reason to believe from his speech and conduct that he hit upon the key before October or November. He never stated, though, whether or not he had succeeded.

But of greatest immediate interest was the Orne material. It took Ward only a short time to prove from identity of penmanship a thing he had already considered established from the text of the letter to Curwen; namely, that Simon Orne and his supposed son were one and the same person. As Orne had said to his correspondent, it was hardly safe to live too long in Salem, hence he resorted to a thirty-year sojourn abroad, and did not return to claim his lands except as a representative of a new generation. Orne had apparently been careful to destroy most of his correspondence, but the citizens who took action in 1771 found and preserved a few letters and papers which excited their wonder. There were cryptic formulae and diagrams in his and other hands which Ward now either copied with care or had photographed, and one extremely mysterious letter in a chirography that the searcher recognised from items in the Registry of Deeds as positively Joseph Curwen's.

This Curwen letter, though undated as to the year, was evidently not the one in answer to which Orne had written the confiscated missive; and from internal evidence Ward placed it not much later than 1750. It may not be amiss to give the text in full, as a sample of the style of one whose history was so dark and terrible. The recipient is addressed as "Simon", but a line (whether drawn by Curwen or Orne Ward could not tell) is run through the word.

"Providence, 1. May

Brother:–

My honour'd Antient Friende, due Respects and earnest Wishes to Him whom we serue for yr eternall Power. I am just come upon That which you ought to knowe, concern'g the Matter of the Laste Extremitie and what to doe regard'g yt. I am not dispos'd to followe you in go'g Away on acct. of my Yeares, for Prouidence hath not ye Sharpeness of ye Bay in hunt'g oute uncommon Things and bringinge to Tryall. I am ty'd up in Shippes and Goodes, and cou'd not doe as you did, besides the Whiche my Farme at Patuxet hath under it What you Knowe, and wou'd not waite for my com'g Backe as an Other.

But I am unreadie for harde Fortunes, as I haue tolde you, and haue longe work'd upon ye Way of get'g Backe after ye Laste. I laste Night strucke on ye Wordes that bringe up YOGGE-SOTHOTHE, and sawe for ye first Time that Face spoke of by Ibn Schacabao in ye —————. And IT said, that ye III Psalme in ye Liber-Damnatus holdes ye Clauicle. With Sunne in V House, Saturne in Trine, drawe ye Pentagram of Fire, and saye ye ninth Uerse thrice. This Uerse repeate eache Roodemas and Hallow's Eue; and ye Thing will breede in ye Outside Spheres.

And of ye Seede of Olde shal One be borne who shal looke Backe, tho' know'g not what he seekes.

Yett will this auaile Nothing if there be no Heir, and if the Saltes, or the Way to make the Saltes, bee not Readie for his Hande; and here I will owne, I haue not taken needed Stepps nor founde Much. Ye Process is plaguy harde to come neare; and it used up such a Store of Specimens, I am harde putte to it to get Enough, notwithstand'g the Sailors I haue from ye Indies. Ye People aboute are become curious, but I can stande them off. Ye Gentry are worse that the Populace, be'g more Circumstantiall in their Accts. and more belieu'd in what they tell. That Parson and Mr. Merritt haue talk'd Some, I am fearfull, but no Thing soe far is Dangerous. Ye Chymical Substances are easie of get'g, there be'g II. goode Chymists in Towne, Dr, Bowen and Sam: Carew. I am foll'g oute what Borellus saith, and haue Helpe in Abdool Al-Hazred his VII. Booke. Whateuer I gette, you shal haue. And in ye meane while, do not neglect to make use of ye Wordes I haue here giuen. I haue them Righte, but if you Desire to see HIM, imploy the Writings on ye Piece of ———— that I am putt'g in this Packet. Saye ye Uerses euery Roodmas and Hallow's Eue; and if ye Line runn out not, *one shal bee in yeares to come that shal looke backe and use what Saltes or Stuff for Saltes you shal leaue him.* Job XIV. XIV.

I rejoice you are again at Salem, and hope I may see you not longe hence. I haue a goode Stallion, and am think'g of get'g a Coach, there be'g one (Mr. Merritt's) in Prouidence already, tho' ye Roades are bad. If you are dispos'd to Trauel, doe not pass me bye. From Boston take ye Post Rd. thro' Dedham, Wrentham, and Attleborough, goode Tauerns be'g at all these Townes. Stop at Mr. Balcom's in Wrentham, where ye Beddes are finer than Mr. Hatch's, but eate at ye other House for their Cooke is better. Turne into Prou. by Patucket Falls, and ye Rd. past Mr. Sayles's Tauern. My House opp. Mr. Epenetus Olney's Tauern off ye Towne Street, Ist on ye N. side of Olney's Court. Distance from Boston Stone abt. XLIV Miles.

Sir, I am ye olde and true Friend and Serut. in Almonsin-Metraton.

Josephus C.

To Mr. Simon Orne,
William's-Lane, in Salem."

This letter, oddly enough, was what first gave Ward the exact location of Curwen's Providence home; for none of the records encountered up to that time had been at all specific. The discovery was doubly striking because it indicated as the newer Curwen house, built in 1761 on the site of the old, a dilapidated building still standing in Olney Court and well known to Ward in his antiquarian rambles over Stampers' Hill. The place was indeed only a few squares from his own home on the great hill's higher ground, and was now the abode of a negro family much esteemed for occasional washing, housecleaning, and furnace-tending services. To find, in distant Salem, such sudden proof of the significance of this familiar rookery in his own family history, was a highly impressive thing to Ward; and he resolved to explore the place immediately upon his return. The more mystical phases of the letter, which he took to be some extravagant kind of symbolism, frankly baffled him; though he noted with a thrill of curiousity that the Biblical passage referred to − Job 14,14 − was the familiar verse, 'If a man die, shall he live again? All the days of my appointed time will I wait, until my change come.'

2

Young Ward came home in a state of pleasant excitement, and spent the following Saturday in a long and exhaustive study of the house in Olney Court. The place, now crumbling with age, had never been a mansion; but was a modest two-and-a-half story wooden town house of the familiar Providence colonial type, with plain peaked roof, large central chimney, and artistically carved doorway with rayed fanlight, triangular pediment, and trim Doric pilasters. It had suffered but little alteration externally, and Ward felt he was gazing on something very close to the sinister matters of his quest.

The present negro inhabitants were known to him, and he was very courteously shewn about the interior by old Asa and his stout wife Hannah. Here there was more change than the outside indicated, and Ward saw with regret that fully half of the fine scroll-and-urn overmantels and shell-carved cupboard linings were gone, whilst most of the fine wainscotting and bolection moulding was marked, hacked, and gouged, or covered up altogether with cheap wall-paper. In general, the survey did not yield as much as Ward had somehow expected; but it was at least exciting to stand within the ancestral walls which had housed such a man of horror as Joseph Curwen. He saw with a thrill that a monogram had been very carefully effaced from the ancient brass knocker.

From then until after the close of school Ward spent his time on the photostatic copy of the Hutchinson cipher and the accumulation of local Curwen data. The former still proved unyielding; but of the latter he obtained so much, and so many clues to similar data elsewhere, that he was ready by July to make a trip to New London and New York to consult old letters whose presence in those places was indicated. This trip was very fruitful, for it brought him the Fenner letters with their terrible description of the Pawtuxet farmhouse raid, and the Nightingale-Talbot letters in which he learned of the portrait painted on a panel of the Curwen library. This matter of the portrait interested him particularly, since he would have given much to know just what Joseph Curwen looked like; and he decided to make a second search of the house in Olney Court to see if there might not be some trace of the ancient features beneath peeling coats of later paint or layers of mouldy wall-paper.

Early in August that search took place, and Ward went carefully over the walls of every room sizeable enough to have been by any possibility the library of the evil builder. He paid especial attention to the large panels of such overmantels as still remained; and was keenly excited after about an hour, when on a broad area above the fireplace in a spacious ground-floor room he became certain that the surface brought out by the peeling of several coats of paint was sensibly darker than any ordinary interior paint or the wood beneath it was likely to have been. A few more careful tests with a thin knife, and he knew that he had come upon an oil portrait of great extent. With truly scholarly restraint the youth did not risk the damage which an immediate attempt to uncover the hidden picture with the knife might have been, but just retired from the scene of his discovery to enlist expert help. In three days he returned with an artist of long experience, Mr. Walter C. Dwight, whose studio is near the foot of College Hill; and that accomplished restorer of paintings set to work at once with proper methods and chemical substances. Old Asa and his wife were duly excited over their strange visitors, and were properly reimbursed for this invasion of their domestic hearth.

As day by the day the work of restoration progressed, Charles Ward looked on with growing interest at the lines and shades gradually unveiled after their long oblivion. Dwight had begun at the bottom; hence since the picture was a three-quarter-length one, the face did not come out for some time. It was meanwhile seen that the subject was a spare, well-shaped man with dark-blue coat, embroidered waistcoat, black satin small-clothes, and white silk stockings, seated in a carved chair against the background of a window with wharves and ships beyond. When the head came out it was observed to bear a neat Albemarle wig, and to

68

possess a thin, calm, undistinguished face which seemed somehow familiar to both Ward and the artist. Only at the very last, though, did the restorer and his client begin to grasp with astonishment at the details of that lean, pallid visage, and to recognise with a touch of awe the dramatic trick which heredity had played. For it took the final bath of oil and the final stroke of the delicate scraper to bring out fully the expression which centuries had hidden; and to confront the bewildered Charles Dexter Ward, dweller in the past, with his own living features in the countenance of his horrible great-great-great-grandfather.

Ward brought his parents to see the marvel he had uncovered, and his father at once determined to purchase the picture despite its execution on stationary panelling. The resemblance to the boy, despite an appearance of rather great age, was marvellous; and it could be seen that through some trick of atavism the physical contours of Joseph Curwen had found precise duplication after a century and a half. Mrs. Ward's resemblance to her ancestor was not at all marked, though she could recall relatives who had some of the facial characteristics shared by her son and by the bygone Curwen. She did not relish the discovery, and told her husband that he had better burn the picture instead of bringing it home. There was, she averred, something unwholesome about it; not only intrinsically, but in its very resemblance to Charles. Mr. Ward, however, was a practical man of power and affairs – a cotton manufacturer with extensive mills at Riverpoint in the Pawtuxet Valley – and not one to listen to feminine scruples. The picture impressed him mightily with its likeness to his son, and he believed the boy deserved it as a present. In this opinion, it is needless to say, Charles most heartily concurred; and a few days later Mr. Ward located the owner of the house – a small rodent-featured person with a guttural accent – and obtained the whole mantel and overmantel bearing the picture at a curtly fixed price which cut short the impending torrent of unctuous haggling.

It now remained to take off the panelling and remove it to the Ward home, where provisions were made for its thorough restoration and installation with an electric mock-fireplace in Charles's third-floor study or library. To Charles was left the task of superintending this removal, and on the twenty-eighth of August he accompanied two expert workmen from the Crooker decorating firm to the house in Olney Court, where the mantel and portrait-bearing overmantel were detached with great care and precision for transportation in the company's motor truck. There was left a space of exposed brickwork marking the chimney's course, and in this young Ward observed a cubical recess about a foot square, which must have lain directly behind the head of the portrait. Curious as to what such a space might mean or contain, the youth approached and looked within; finding beneath the deep coatings of dust and soot some loose yellowed papers, a crude, thick copybook, and a few mouldering textile shreds which may have formed the ribbon binding the rest together. Blowing away the bulk of the dirt and cinders, he took up the book and looked at the bold inscription on its cover. It was in a hand which he had learned to recognise at the Essex Institute, and proclaimed the volume as the *Journall and Notes of Jos: Curwen, Gent. of Prouidence-Plantations, Late of Salem.*'

Excited beyond measure by his discovery, Ward shewed the book to the two curious workmen beside him. Their testimony is absolute as to the nature and genuineness of the finding, and Dr. Willett relies on them to help establish his theory that the youth was not mad when he began his major eccentricities. All the other papers were likewise in Curwen's handwriting, and one of them seemed especially portentous because of its inscription: *'To Him Who Shal Come After, & How He May Gett Beyonde Time & Ye Spheres.'*

Another was in a cipher; the same, Ward hoped, as the Hutchinson cipher which had hitherto baffled him. A third, and here the searcher rejoiced, seemed to be a key to the cipher; whilst the fourth and fifth were addressed respectively to:'Edw: Hutchinson, Armiger' and Jedediah Orne, esq.', 'or Their Heir or Heirs, or Those Represent'g Them.' The sixth and last was inscribed: *Joseph Curwen his Life and Travells Bet'n ye yeares 1678 and 1687: Of Whither He Voyag'd, Where He Stay'd, Whom He Sawe, and What He Learnt.'*

3

We have now reached the point from which the more academic school of alienists date Charles Ward's madness. Upon his discovery the youth had looked immediately at a few of the inner pages of the book and manuscripts, and had evidently seen something which impressed him tremendously. Indeed, in shewing the titles to the workmen, he appeared to guard the text itself with peculiar care, and to labour under a perturbation for which even the antiquarian and genealogical significance of the find could hardly account. Upon returning home he broke the news with an almost embarrassed air, as if he wished to convey an idea of its supreme importance without having to exhibit the evidence itself. He did not even shew the titles to his parents, but simply told them that he had found some documents in Joseph Curwen's handwriting, 'mostly in cipher', which would have to be studied very carefully before yielding up their true meaning. It is unlikely that he would have shewn what he did to the workmen, had it not been for their unconcealed curiousity. As it was he doubtless wished to avoid any display of peculiar reticence which would increase their discussion of the matter.

That night Charles Ward sat up in his room reading the new-found book and papers, and when day came he did not desist. His meals, on his urgent request when his mother called to see what was amiss, were sent up to him; and in the afternoon he appeared only briefly when the men came to install the Curwen picture and mantelpiece in his study. The next night he slept in snatches in his clothes, meanwhile wrestling feverishly with the unravelling of the cipher manuscript. In the morning his mother saw that he was at work on the photostatic copy of the Hutchinson cipher, which he had frequently shewn her before; but in response to her query he said that the Curwen key could not be applied to it. That afternoon he abandoned his work and watched the men fascinatedly as they finished their installation of the picture with its woodwork above a cleverly realistic electric log, setting the mock-fireplace and overmantel a little out from the north wall as if a chimney existed, and boxing in the sides with panelling to match the room's. The front panel holding the picture was sawn and hinged to allow cupboard space behind it. After the workmen went he moved his work into the study and sat down before it with his eyes half on the cipher and half on the portrait which stared back at him like a year-adding and century-recalling mirror.

His parents, subsequently recalling his conduct at this period, give interesting details anent the policy of concealment which he practised. Before servants he seldom hid any paper which he might by studying, since he rightly assumed that Curwen's intricate and archaic chirography would be too much for them.

With his parents, however, he was more circumspect; and unless the manuscript in question were a cipher, or a mere mass of cryptic symbols and unknown ideographs (as that entitled *To Him Who Shal Come After, etc.*' seemed to be), he would cover it with some convenient paper until his caller had departed. At night he kept the papers under lock and key in an antique cabinet of his, where he also placed them whenever he left the room. He soon resumed fairly regular hours and habits, except that his long walks and other outside interests seemed to cease. The opening of school, where he now began his senior year, seemed a great bore to him; and he frequently asserted his determination never to bother with college. He had, he said, important special investigations to make, which would provide him with more avenues toward knowledge and the humanities than any university which the world could boast.

Naturally, only one who had always been more or less studious, eccentric, and solitary could have pursued this course for many days without attracting notice. Ward, however, was constitutionally a scholar and a hermit; hence his parents were less surprised than regretful at the close confinement and secrecy he adopted. At the same time, both his father and mother thought it odd that he would shew them no scrap of his treasure-trove, nor give any connected account of such data as he had deciphered. This reticence he explained away as due to a wish to wait until he might announce some connected revelation, but as the weeks passed without further disclosures there began to grow up between the youth and his family a kind of constraint; intensified in his mother's case by her manifest disapproval of all Curwen delvings.

During October Ward began visiting the libraries again, but no longer for the antiquarian matter of his former days. Witchcraft and magic, occultism and daemonology, were what he sought now; and when Providence sources proved unfruitful he would take the train for Boston and tap the wealth of the great library in Copley Square, the Widener Library at Harvard, or the Zion Research Library in Brookline, where certain rare works on Biblical subjects are available. He bought extensively, and fitted up a whole additional set of shelves in his study for newly acquired works on uncanny subjects; while during the Christmas holidays he made a round of out-of-town trips including one to Salem to consult certain records at the Essex Institute.

About the middle of January, 1920, there entered Ward's bearing an element of triumph which he did not explain, and he was no more found at work upon the Hutchinson cipher. Instead, he inaugurated a dual policy of chemical research and record-scanning; fitting up for the one a laboratory in the unused attic of the house, and for the latter haunting all the sources of vital statistics in Providence. Local dealers in drugs and scientific supplies, later questioned, gave astonishingly queer and meaningless catalogues of the substances and instruments he purchased; but clerks at the State House, the City Hall, and the various libraries agree as to the definite object of his second interest. He was searching intensely and feverishly for the grave of Joseph Curwen, from whose slate slab an older generation had so wisely blotted the name.

Little by little there grew upon the Ward family the conviction that something was wrong. Charles had had freaks and changes of minor interests before, but this growing secrecy and absorption in strange pursuits was unlike even him. His school work was the merest pretence; and although he failed in no test, it could be seen that the older application had all vanished. He had other concernments now; and when not in his new laboratory with a score of obsolete alchemical books, could be found either poring over old burial records down town or glued to his volumes of occult lore in his study, where the startlingly – one almost fancied increasingly – similar features of Joseph Curwen stared blandly at him from the great overmantel on the North wall.

Late in March Ward added to his archive-searching a ghoulish series of rambles about the various ancient cemeteries of the city. The cause appeared later, when it was learned from City Hall clerks that he had probably found an important clue. His quest had suddenly shifted from the grave of Joseph Curwen to that of one Naphthali Field; and this shift was explained when, upon going over the files that he had been over, the investigators actually found a fragmentary record of Curwen's burial which had escaped the general obliteration, and which stated that the curious leaden coffin had been interred '10 ft. S. and 5 ft. W. of Naphthali Field's grave in y-.' The lack of a specified burying-ground in the surviving entry greatly complicated the search, and Naphthali Field's grave seemed as elusive as that of Curwen; but here no systematic effacement had existed, and one might reasonably be expected to stumble on the stone itself even if its record had perished. Hence the rambles – from which St. John's (the former King's) Churchyard and the ancient Congregational burying-ground in the midst of Swan Point Cemetery were excluded, since other statistics had shewn that the only Naphthali Field (obit. 1729) whose grave could have been meant had been a Baptist.

4

It was toward May when Dr. Willett, at the request of the senior Ward, and fortified with all the Curwen data which the family had gleaned from Charles in his non-secretive days, talked with the young man. The interview was of little value or conclusiveness, for

Willett felt at every moment that Charles was thorough master of himself and in touch with matters of real importance; but it at least force the secretive youth to offer some rational explanation of his recent demeanour. Of a pallid, impassive type not easily shewing embarrassment, Ward seemed quite ready to discuss his pursuits, though not to reveal their object. He stated that the papers of his ancestor had contained some remarkable secrets of early scientific knowledge, for the most part in cipher, of an apparent scope comparable only to the discoveries of Friar Bacon and perhaps surpassing even those. They were, however, meaningless except when correlated with a body of learning now wholly obsolete; so that their immediate presentation to a world equipped only with modern science would rob them of all impressiveness and dramatic significance. To take their vivid place in the history of human thought they must first be correlated by one familiar with the background out of which they evolved, and to this task of correlation Ward was now devoting himself. He was seeking to acquire as fast as possible those neglected arts of old which a true interpreter of the Curwen data must possess, and hoped in time to made a full announcement and presentation of the utmost interest to mankind and to the world of thought. Not even Einstein, he declared, could more profoundly revolutionise the current conception of things.

As to his graveyard search, whose object he freely admitted, but the details of whose progress he did not relate, he said he had reason to think that Joseph Curwen's mutilated headstone bore certain mystic symbols – carved from directions in his will and ignorantly spared by those who had effaced the name – which were absolutely essential to the final solution of his cryptic system. Curwen, he believed, had wish to guard his secret with care; and had consequently distributed the data in an exceedingly curious fashion. When Dr. Willett asked to see the mystic documents, Ward displayed much reluctance and tried to put him off with such things as photostatic copies of the Hutchinson cipher and Orne formulae and diagrams; but finally shewed him the exteriors of some of the real Curwen finds – the '*Journall and Notes*', the cipher (title in cipher also), and the formula-filled message '*To Him Who Shal Come After*' – and let him glance inside such as were in obscure characters.

He also opened the diary at a page carefully selected for its innocuousness and gave Willett a glimpse of Curwen's connected handwriting in English. The doctor noted very closely the crabbed and complicated letters, and the general aura of the seventeenth century which clung round both penmanship and style despite the writer's survival into the eighteenth century, and became quickly certain that the document was genuine. The text itself was relatively trivial, and Willett recalled only a fragment:

"Wedn. 16 Octr. 1754. My Sloope the Wakeful this Day putt in from London with XX newe Men pick'd up in ye Indies, Spaniards from Martineco and 2 Dutch Men from Surinam. Ye Dutch Men are like to Desert from have'g hearde Somewhat ill of these Ventures, but I will see to ye Inducing of them to Staye. For Mr. Knight Dexter of ye Bay and Book 120 Pieces Camblets, 100 Pieces Assrtd. Cambleteens, 20 Pieces blue Duffles, 100 Pieces Shalloons, 50 Pieces Calamancoes, 300 Pieces each, Shendsoy and Humhums. For Mr. Green at ye Elephant 50 Gallon Cyttles, 20 Warm'g Pannes, 15 Bake Cyttles, 10 pr. Smoke'g Tonges. For Mr. Perrigo 1 Sett of Awles. For Mr. Nightingale 50 Reames prime Foolscap. Say'd ye SABAOTH thrice last Nighte but None appear'd. I must heare more from Mr. H. in Transylvania, tho' it is Harde reach'g him and exceeding strange he can not give me the Use of What he hath so well us'd these hundred Yeares. Simon hath not writ these V. Weekes, but I expecte soon hear'g from Him."

When upon reaching this point Dr. Willett turned the leaf he was quickly checked by Ward, who almost snatched the book from his grasp. All that the doctor had a chance to see on the newly opened page was a brief pair of sentences; but these, strangely enough, lingered tenacious in his memory. They ran: "Ye Verse from Liber-Damnatus be'g spoke V Roodmasses and IV Hallows-Eves, I am Hopeful ye Thing is breed'g Outside ye Spheres. It will drawe One who is to Come, if I can make sure he shal Bee, and he shal think on Past Thinges and look back thro' all ye Yeares, against ye Which I must have ready ye Saltes or That to make 'em with."

Willett saw no more, but somehow this small glimpse gave a new and vague terror to the painted features of Joseph Curwen which stared blandly down from the overmantel. Even after that he entertained the odd fancy – which his medical skill of course assured him was only a fancy – that the eyes of the portrait had a sort of wish, if not an actual tendency, to follow young Charles Ward as he move about the room. He stopped before leaving to study the picture closely, marvelling at its resemblance to Charles and memorising every minute detail of the cryptical, colourless face, even down to a slight scar or pit in the smooth brow above the right eye. Cosmo Alexander, he decided, was a painter worthy of the Scotland that produced Raeburn, and a teacher worthy of his illustrious pupil Gilbert Stuart.

Assured by the doctor that Charles's mental health was in no danger, but that on the other hand he was engaged in researches which might prove of real importance, the Wards were more lenient than they might otherwise have been when during the following June the youth made positive his refusal to attend college. He had, he declared, studies of much more vital importance to pursue; and intimated a wish to go abroad the following year in order to avail himself of certain sources of data not existing in America. The senior Ward, while denying this latter wish as absurd for a boy of only eighteen, acquiesced regarding the university; so that after a none too brilliant graduation from the Moses Brown School there ensued for Charles a three-year period of intensive occult study and graveyard searching. He became recognised as an eccentric, and dropped even more completely from the sight of his family's friends than he had been before; keeping close to his work and only occasionally making trips to other cities to consult obscure records. Once he went south to talk to a strange mulatto who dwelt in a swamp and about whom a newspaper hand printed a curious article. Again he sought a small village in the Adirondacks whence reports of certain odd ceremonial practices had come. But still his parents forbade him the trip to the Old World which he desired.

Coming of age in April, 1923, and having previously inherited a small competence from his maternal grandfather, Ward determined at last to take the European trip hitherto denied him. Of his proposed itinerary he would say nothing save that the needs of his studies would carry him to many places, but he promised to write his parents fully and faithfully. When they saw he could not be dissuaded, they ceased all opposition and helped as best they could; so that in June the young man sailed for Liverpool with the farewell blessings of his father and mother, who accompanied him to Boston and waved him out of sight from the White Star pier in Charlestown. Letters soon told of his safe arrival, and of his securing good quarters in Great Russell Street, London; where he proposed to stay, shunning all family friends, till he had exhausted the resources of the British Museum in a certain direction. Of his daily life he wrote by little, for there was little to write. Study and experiment consumed all his time, and he mentioned a laboratory which he had established in one of his rooms. That he said nothing of antiquarian rambles in the glamorous old city with its luring skyline of ancient domes and steeples and its tangles of roads and alleys whose mystic convolutions and sudden vistas alternately beckon and surprise, was taken by his parents as a good index of the degree to which his new interests had engrossed his mind.

In June, 1924, a brief note told of his departure for Paris, to which he had before made one or two flying trips for material in the Bibliothèque Nationale. For three months thereafter he sent only postal cards, giving an address in the Rue St. Jacques and referring to a special search among rare manuscripts in the library of an unnamed private collector. He avoided acquaintances, and no tourists brought back reports of having seen him. Then came a silence, and in October the Wards received a picture card from Prague, Czecho-Slovakia, stating that Charles was in that ancient town for the purpose of conferring with a certain very aged man supposed to be the last living possessor of some very curious mediaeval information. He gave an address in the Neustadt, and announced no move till the following January; when he dropped several cards from Vienna telling of his passage through that city on the way toward a more easterly region whither one of his correspondents and fellow-delvers into the occult had invited him.

The next card was from Klausenburg in Transylvania, and told of Ward's progress toward his destination. He was going to visit a Baron Ferenczy, whose estate lay in the mountains east of Rakus; and was to be addressed at Rakus in the care of that nobleman.

Another card from Rakus a week later, saying that his host's carriage had met him and that he was leaving the village for the mountains, was his last message for a considerable time; indeed, he did reply to his parents' frequent letters until May, when he wrote to discourage the plan of his mother for a meeting in London, Paris, or Rome during the summer, when the elder Wards were planning to travel to Europe. His researches, he said, were such that he could not leave his present quarters; while the situation of Baron Ferenczy's castle did not favour visits. It was on a crag in the dark wooded mountains, and the region was so shunned by the country folk that normal people could not help feeling ill at ease. Moreover, the Baron was not a person likely to appeal to correct and conservative New England gentlefolk. His aspect and manners had idiosyncrasies, and his age was so great as to be disquieting. It would be better, Charles said, if his parents would wait for his return to Providence; which could scarcely be far distant.

That return did not, however, take place until May 1926, when after a few heralding cards the young wanderer quietly slipped into New York on the *Homeric* and traversed the long miles to Providence by motor-coach, eagerly drinking in the green rolling hills, and fragrant, blossoming orchards, and the white steepled towns of vernal Connecticut; his first taste of ancient New England in nearly four years. When the coach crossed the Pawcatuck and entered Rhode Island amidst the faery goldenness of a late spring afternoon his heart beat with quickened force, and the entry to Providence along Reservoir and Elmwood Avenues was a breathless and wonderful thing despite the depths of forbidden lore to which he had delved. At the high square where Broad, Weybosset, and Empire Streets join, he saw before and below him in the fire of sunset the pleasant, remembered houses and domes and steeples of the old town; and his head swam curiously as the vehicle rolled down to the terminal behind the Biltmore, bringing into view the great dome and soft, roof-pierced greenery of the ancient hill across the river, and the tall colonial spire of the First Baptist Church limned pink in the magic evening against the fresh springtime verdure of its precipitous background.

Old Providence! It was this place and the mysterious forces of its long, continuous history which had brought him into being, and which had drawn him back toward marvels and secrets whose boundaries no prophet might fix. Here lay the arcana, wondrous or dreadful as the case may be, for which all his years of travel and application had been preparing him. A taxicab whirled him through Post Office Square with its glimpse of the river, the old Market House, and the head of the bay, and up the steep curved slope of Waterman Street to Prospect, where the vast gleaming dome and sunset-flushed Ionic columns of the Christian Science Church beckoned northward. Then eight squares past the fine old estates his childish eyes had known, and the quaint brick sidewalks so often trodden by his youthful feet. And at last the little white overtaken farmhouse on the right, on the left the classic Adam porch and stately facade of the great brick house where he was born. It was twilight, and Charles Dexter Ward had come home.

5

A school of alienists slightly less academic than Dr. Lyman's assign to Ward's European trip the beginning of his true madness. Admitting that he was sane when he started, they believe that his conduct upon returning implies a disastrous change. But even to this claim Dr. Willett refuses to concede. There was, he insists, something later; and the queerness of the youth at this stage he attributes to the practice of rituals learned abroad – odd enough things, to be sure, but by no means implying mental aberration on the part of their celebrant. Ward himself, though visibly aged and hardened, was still normal in his general reactions; and in several talks with Dr. Willett displayed a balance which no madman – even an incipient one – could feign continuously for long. What elicited the notion of insanity at this period were the *sounds* heard at all hours from Ward's attic laboratory, in which he kept himself most of the time. There were chantings and repetitions, and thunderous declamations in uncanny rhythms; and although these sounds were always in Ward's own voice, there was something in the quality of that voice, and in the accents of the formulae it pronounced, which could not by chill the blood of every hearer. It was noticed that Nig, the venerable and beloved black cat of the household, bristled and arched his back perceptibly when certain of the tones were heard.

The odours occasionally wafted from the laboratory were likewise exceedingly strange. Sometimes they were very noxious, but more often they were aromatic, with a haunting, elusive quality which seemed to have the power of inducing fantastic images. People who smelled them had a tendency to glimpse momentary mirages of enormous vistas, with strange hills or endless avenues of sphinxes and hippogriffs stretching off into infinite distance. Ward did not resume his old-time rambles, but applied himself diligently to the strange books he had brought home, and to equally strange delvings within his quarters; explaining that European sources had greatly enlarged the possibilities of his work, and promising great revelations in the years to come. His older aspect increased to a startling degree his resemblance to the Curwen portrait in his library; and Dr. Willett would often pause by the latter after a call, marvelling at the virtual identity, and reflecting that only the small pit above the picture's right eye now remained to differentiate the long-dead wizard from the living youth. These calls of Willett's, undertaken at the request of teh senior Wards, were curious affairs. Ward at no time repulsed the doctor, but the latter saw that he could never reach the young man's inner psychology. Frequently he noted peculiar things about; little wax images of grotesque design on the shelves or tables, and the half-erased remnants of circles, triangles, and pentagrams in chalk or charcoal on the cleared central space of the large room. And always in the night those rhythms and incantations thundered, till it became very difficult to keep servants or suppress furtive talk of Charles's madness.

In January, 1927, a peculiar incident occurred. One night about midnight, as Charles was chanting a ritual whose weird cadence echoed unpleasantly through the house below, there came a sudden gust of chill wind from the bay, and a faint, obscure trembling of the earth which everyone in the neighbourhood noted. At the same time the cat exhibited phenomenal traces of fright, while dogs bayed for as much as a mile around. This was the prelude to a sharp thunderstorm, anomalous for the season, which brought with it such a crash that Mr. and Mrs. Ward believed the house had been struck. They rushed upstairs to see what damage had been done, but Charles met them at the door to the attic; pale, resolute, and portentous, with an almost fearsome combination of triumph and seriousness on his face. He assured them that the house had not really been struck, and that the storm would soon be over. They paused, and looking through a window saw that he was indeed right; for the lightning flashed farther and farther off, whilst the trees ceased to bend in the strange frigid gust from the water. The thunder sank to a sort of dull mumbling chuckle and finally died away. Stars came out, and the stamp of triumph on Charles Ward's face crystallised into a very singular expression.

For two months or more after this incident Ward was less confined than usual to his laboratory. He exhibited a curious interest in the weather, and made odd inquires about the date of the spring thawing of the ground. One night late in March he left the house after midnight, and did not return till almost morning; when his mother, being wakeful, heard a rumbling motor draw up to the carriage entrance. Muffled oaths could be distinguished, and Mrs. Ward, rising and going to the window, saw four dark figures removing a long, heavy box from a truck at Charles's direction and carrying it within by the side door. She heard laboured breathing and ponderous footfalls on the stairs, and finally a dull thumping in the attic; after which the footfalls descended again, and the four reappeared outside and drove off in their truck.

The next day Charles resumed his strict attic seclusion, drawing down the dark shades of his laboratory windows and appearing to be working on some metal substance. He would open the door to no one, and steadfastly refused all proffered food. About noon a wrenching sound followed by a terrible cry and a fall were heard, but when Mrs. Ward rapped at the door her son at length answered faintly, and told her that nothing had gone amiss. The hideous and indescribable stench now welling out was absolutely harmless and unfortunately necessary. Solitude was the one prime essential, and he would appear later for dinner. That afternoon, after the conclusion of some odd hissing sounds which came from behind the locked portal, he did finally appear; wearing an extremely haggard aspect and forbidding anyone to enter the laboratory upon any pretext. This, indeed, proved the beginning of a new policy of secrecy; for never afterward was any other person permitted to visit either the mysterious garret workroom or the adjacent storeroom which he cleaned out, furnished roughly, and added to his inviolable private domain as a sleeping apartment. Here he lived, with books brought up from his library beneath, till the time he purchased the Pawtuxet bungalow and moved to it all his scientific effects.

In the evening Charles secured the paper before the rest of the family and damaged part of it through an apparent accident. Later on Dr. Willett, having fixed the date from statements by various members of the household, looked up an intact copy at the *Journal* office and found that in the destroyed section the following small item had occurred:

Nocturnal Diggers Surprised in North Burial Ground

Robert Hart, night watchman at the North Burial Ground, this morning discovered a party of several men with a motor truck in the oldest part of the cemetery, but apparently frightened them off before they had accomplished whatever their object may have been.

The discovery took place at about four o'clock, when Hart's attention was attracted by the sound of a motor outside his shelter. Investigating, he saw a large truck on the main drive several rods away; but could not reach it before the noise of his feet on the gravel had revealed his approach. The men hastily placed a large box in the truck and drove away toward the street before they could be overtaken; and since no known grave was disturbed, Hart believes that this box was an object which they wished to bury.

The diggers must have been at work for a long while before detection, for Hart found an enormous hold dug at a considerable distance back from the roadway in the lot of Amasa Field, where most of the old stones have long ago disappeared. The hole, a place as large and deep as a grave, was empty; and did

86

not coincide with any interment mentioned in the cemetery records.

Sergt. Riley of the Second Station viewed the spot and gave the opinion that the hole was dug by bootleggers rather gruesomely and ingeniously seeking a safe cache for liquor in a place not likely to be disturbed. In reply to questions Hart said he though the escaping truck had headed up Rochambeau Avenue, though he could not be sure.

During the next few days Charles Ward was seldom seen by his family. Having added sleeping quarters to his attic realm, he kept closely to himself there, ordering food brought to the door and not taking it in until after the servant had gone away. The droning of monotonous formulae and the chanting of bizarre rhythms recurred at intervals, while at other times occasional listeners could detect the sound of tinkling glass, hissing chemicals, running water, or roaring gas flames. Odours of the most unplaceable quality, wholly unlike any before noted, hung at times around the door; and the air of tension observable in the young recluse whenever he did venture briefly forth was such as to excite the keenest speculation. Once he made a hasty trip to the Athenaeum for a book he required, and again he hired a messenger to fetch him a highly obscure volume from Boston. Suspense was written portentously over the whole situation, and both the family and Dr. Willett confessed themselves wholly at a loss what to do or think about it.

6

Then on the fifteenth of April a strange development occurred. While nothing appeared to grow different in kind, there was certainly a very terrible difference in degree; and Dr. Willett somehow attaches great significance to the change. The day was

Good Friday, a circumstance of which the servants made much, but which others quite naturally dismiss as an irrelevant coincidence. Late in the afternoon young Ward began repeating a certain formula in a singularly loud voice, at the same time burning some substance so pungent that its fumes escaped over the entire house. The formula was so plainly audible in the hall outside the locked door that Mrs. Ward could not help memorising it as she waited and listened anxiously, and later on she was able to write it down at Dr. Willett's request. It ran as follows, and experts have told Dr. Willett that its very close analogue can be found in the mystic writings of "Eliphas Levi", that cryptic soul who crept through a crack in the forbidden door and glimpsed the frightful vistas of the void beyond:

"Per Adonai Eloim, Adonai Jehova,
Adonai Sabaoth, Metraton On Agla Mathon,
verbum pythonicum, mysterium salamandrae,
conventus sylvorum, antra gnomorum,
daemonia Coeli God, Almonsin, Gibor, Jehosua,
Evam, Zariatnatmik, veni, veni, veni."

This had been going on for two hours without change or intermission when over all the neighbourhood a pandaemoniac howling of dogs set in. The extent of this howling can be judged from the space it received in the papers the next day, but to those in the Ward household it was overshadowed by the odour which instantly followed it; a hideous, all-pervasive odour which non of them had ever smelt before or have ever smelt since. In the midst of this mephitic flood there came a very perceptible flash like that of lightning, which would have been blinding and impressive but for the daylight around; and then was heard *the voice* that no listener can

88

ever forget because of its thunderous remoteness, its incredible depth, and its eldritch dissimilarity to Charles Ward's voice. It shook the house, and was clearly heard by at least two neighbours above the howling of the dogs. Mrs. Ward, who had been listening in despair outside her son's locked laboratory, shivered as she recognised its hellish imports; for Charles had told of its evil fame in dark books, and of the manner in which it had thundered, according to the Fenner letter, above the doomed Pawtuxet farmhouse on the night of Joseph Curwen's annihilation. There was no mistaking that nightmare phrase, for Charles had described it too vividly in the old days when he had talked frankly of his Curwen investigations. And yet it was only this fragment of an archaic and forgotten language: 'DIES MIES JESCHET BOENE DOESEF DOUVEMA ENITEMAUS.'

Close upon this thundering there came a momentary darkening of the daylight, though sunset was still an hour distant, and then a puff of added odour different from the first but equally unknown and intolerable. Charles was chanting again now and his mother could hear syllables that sounded like 'Yi nash Yog Sothoth he lgeb throdag' – ending in a 'Yah!' whose maniacal force mounted in an ear-splitting crescendo. A second later all previous memories were effaced by the wailing scream which burst out with frantic explosiveness and gradually changed form to a paroxysm of diabolic and hysterical laughter. Mrs. Ward, with the mingled fear and blind courage of maternity, advanced and knocked affrightedly at the concealing panels, but obtained no sign of recognition. She knocked again, but paused nervelessly as a second shriek arose, this one unmistakably in the familiar voice of her son, *and sounding concurrently with the still bursting cachinnations of that other voice.* Presently she fainted, although she is still unable to recall the precise and immediate cause. Memory sometimes makes merciful deletions.

Mr. Ward returned from the business section at about quarter past six; and not finding his wife downstairs, was told by the frightened servants that she was probably watching at Charles's door, from which the sounds had been far stranger than ever before. Mounting the stairs at once, he saw Mrs. Ward stretched out at full length on the floor of the corridor outside the laboratory; and realising that she had fainted, hastened to fetch a glass of water from a set bowl in a neighbouring alcove. Dashing the cold fluid in her face, he was heartened to observe an immediate response on her part, and was watching the bewildered opening of her eyes when a chill shot through him and threatened to reduce him to the very state from which she was emerging. For the seemingly silent laboratory was not as silent as it had appeared to be, but held the murmurs of a tense, muffled conversation in tones too low for comprehension, yet of a quality profoundly disturbing to the soul.

It was not, of course, new for Charles to mutter formulae; but this muttering was definitely different. It was so palpably a dialogue, or imitation of a dialogue, with the regular alteration of inflections suggesting question and answer, statement and response. One voice was undisguisedly that of Charles, but the other had a depth and hollowness which the youth's best powers of ceremonial mimicry had scarcely approached before. There was something hideous, blasphemous, and abnormal about it, and but for a cry from his recovering wife which cleared his mind by arousing his protective instincts it is not likely that Theodore Howland Ward could have maintained for nearly a year more his old boast that he had never fainted. As it was, he seized his wife in his arms and bore her quickly downstairs before she could notice the voices which had so horribly disturbed him. Even so, however, he was not quick enough to escape catching something himself which caused him to stagger dangerously with his burden. For Mrs. Ward's cry had evidently been heard by others than he, and there had come in response to it from behind the locked door the first distinguishable words which that masked and terrible colloquy had yielded. They were merely an excited caution in Charles's own voice, but somehow their implications held a nameless fright for the father who overheard them. The phrase was just this: *'Sshh! – write!'*

Mr. and Mrs. Ward conferred at some length after dinner, and the former resolved to have a firm and serious talk with Charles that very night. No matter how important the object, such conduct could no longer be permitted; for these latest developments transcended every limit of sanity and formed a menace to the order and nervous well-being of the entire household. The youth must indeed have taken complete leave of his senses, since only downright madness could have prompted the wild screams and imaginary conversations in assumed voices which the present day had brought forth. All this must be stopped, or Mrs. Ward would be made ill and the keeping of servants become an impossibility.

Mr. Ward rose at the close of the meal and started upstairs for Charles's laboratory. On the third floor, however, he paused at the sounds which he heard proceeding from the now disused library of his son. Books were apparently being flung about and papers wildly rustled, and upon stepping to the door Mr. Ward beheld the youth within, excitedly assembling a vast armful of literary matter of every size and shape. Charles's aspect was very drawn and haggard, and he dropped his entire load with a start at the sound of his father's voice. At the elder man's command he sat down, and for some time listened to the admonitions he had so long deserved. There was no scene. At the end of the lecture he agreed that his father was right, and that his noises, mutterings, incantations, and chemical odours were indeed inexcusable nuisances. He agreed to a policy of great quiet, though insisting on a prolongation of his extreme privacy. Much of his future work, he said, was in any case purely book research; and he could obtain quarters elsewhere for any such vocal rituals as might be necessary at a later stage. For the fright and fainting of his mother he expressed the keenest contrition, and explained that the conversation later heard was part of an elaborate symbolism designed to create a certain mental atmosphere. His use of abstruse technical terms somewhat bewildered Mr. Ward, but the parting impression was one of undeniable sanity and poise despite a mysterious tension of the utmost gravity. The interview was really quite inconclusive, and as Charles picked up his armful and left the room Mr. Ward hardly knew what to make of the entire business. It was as mysterious as the death of poor old Nig, whose stiffening form had been found an hour before in the basement, with staring eyes and fear-distorted mouth.

Driven by some vague detective instinct, the bewildered parent now glanced curiously at the vacant shelves to see what his son had taken up to the attic. The youth's library was plainly and rigidly classified, so that one might tell at a glance the books or at least the kind of books which had been withdrawn. On this occasion Mr. Ward was astonished to find that nothing of the occult or the antiquarian, beyond what had been previously removed, was missing. These new withdrawals were all modern items; histories, scientific treatises, geographies, manuals of literature, philosophic works, and certain contemporary newspapers and magazines. It was a very curious shift from Charles Ward's recent run of reading, and the father paused in a growing vortex of perplexity and an engulfing sense of strangeness. The strangeness was a very poignant sensation, and almost clawed at his chest as he strove to see just what was wrong around him. Something was indeed wrong, and tangibly as well as spiritually so. Ever since he had been in this room he had known that something was amiss, and at last it dawned upon him what it was.

On the north wall rose still the ancient carved overmantel from the house in Olney Court, but to the cracked and precariously restored oils of the large Curwen portrait disaster had come. Time and unequal heating had done their work at last, and at some time since the room's last cleaning the worst had happened. Peeling clear of the wood, curling tighter and tighter, and finally crumbling into small bits with what must have been malignly silent suddenness, the portrait of Joseph Curwen had resigned forever its staring surveillance of the youth it so strangely resembled, and now lay scattered on the floor as a thin coating of fine blue-grey dust.

CHAPTER FOUR

A Mutation and a Madness

1

In the week following that memorable Good Friday Charles Ward was seen more often than usual, and was continually carrying books between his library and the attic laboratory. His actions were quiet and rational, but he had a furtive, hunted look which his mother did not like, and developed an incredibly ravenous appetite as gauged by his demands upon the cook. Dr. Willett had been told of those Friday noises and happenings, and on the following Tuesday had a long conversation with the youth in the library where the picture stared no more. The interview was, as always, inconclusive; but Willett is still ready to swear that the youth was sane and himself at the time. He held out promises of an early revelation, and spoke of the need of securing a laboratory elsewhere. At the loss of the portrait he grieved singularly little considering his first enthusiasm over it, but seemed to find something of positive humour in its sudden crumbling.

About the second week Charles began to be absent from the house for long periods, and one day when good old black Hannah came to help with the spring cleaning she mentioned his frequent visits to the old house in Olney Court, where he would come with a large valise and perform curious delvings in the cellar. He was always very liberal to her and to old Asa, but seemed more worried than he used to be; which grieved her very much, since she had watched him grow up from birth. Another report of his doings came from Pawtuxet, where some friends of the family saw him at a distance a surprising number of times. He seemed to haunt the resort and canoe-house of Rhodes-on-the-Pawtuxet, and subsequent inquiries by Dr. Willett at that place brought out the fact that his purpose was always to secure access to the rather hedged-in river-bank, along which he would walk toward the north, usually not reappearing for a very long while.

Late in May came a momentary revival of ritualistic sounds in the attic laboratory which brought a stern reproof from Mr. Ward and a somewhat distracted promise of amendment from Charles. It occurred one morning, and seemed to form a resumption of the imaginary conversation noted on that turbulent Good Friday. The youth was arguing or remonstrating hotly with himself, for there suddenly burst forth a perfectly distinguishable series of clashing shouts in differentiated tones like alternate demands and denials which caused Mrs. Ward to run upstairs and listen at the door. She could hear no more than a fragment whose only plain words were 'must have it red for three months', and upon her knocking all sounds ceased at once. When Charles was later questioned by his father he said that there were certain conflicts of spheres of consciousness which only great skill could avoid, but which he would try to transfer to other realms.

About the middle of June a queer nocturnal incident occurred. In the early evening there had been some noise and thumping in the laboratory upstairs, and Mr. Ward was on the point of investigating when it suddenly quieted down. That midnight, after the family had retired, the butler was nightlocking the front door when according to his statement Charles appeared somewhat blunderingly and uncertainly at the foot of the stairs with a large suitcase and made signs that he wished egress. The youth spoke no word, but the worthy Yorkshireman caught one sight of his fevered eyes and trembled causelessly. He opened the door and young Ward went out, but in the morning he presented his resignation to Mrs. Ward. There was, he said, something unholy in the glance Charles had fixed on him. It was no way for a young gentleman to look at an honest person, and he could not possibly stay another night. Mrs. Ward allowed the man to depart, but she did not value his statement highly. To fancy Charles in a savage state that night was quite ridiculous, for as long as she had remained awake she had heard faint sounds from the laboratory above; sounds as if of sobbing and pacing, and of a sighing which told only of despair's profoundest depths. Mrs. Ward had grown used to listening for sounds in the night, for the mystery of her son was fast driving all else from her mind.

The next evening, much as on another evening nearly three months before, Charles Ward seized the newspaper very early and accidentally lost the main section. This matter was not recalled till later, when Dr. Willett began checking up loose ends and searching out missing links here and there. In the *Journal* office he found the section which Charles had lost, and marked two items as of possible significance. They were as follows:

More Cemetery Delving

It was this morning discovered by Robert Hart, night watchman at the North Burial Ground, that ghouls were again at work in the ancient portion of the cemetery. The grave of Ezra Weeden, who was born in 1740 and died in 1824 according to his uprooted and savagely splintered slate headstone, was found excavated and rifled, the work being evidently done with a spade stolen from an adjacent tool-shed.

Whatever the contents may have been after more than a century of burial, all was gone except a few slivers of decayed wood. There were no wheel tracks, but the police have measured a single set of footprints which they found in the vicinity, and which indicate the boots of a man of refinement.

Hart is inclined to link this incident with the digging discovered last March, when a party in a motor truck were frightened away after making a deep excavation; but Sergt. Riley of the Second Station discounts this theory and points to vital differences in the two cases. In March the digging had been in a spot where no grave was known; but this time a well-marked and cared-for grave had been rifled with every evidence of deliberate purpose, and with a conscious malignity expressed in the splintering of the slab which had been intact up to the day before.

Members of the Weeden family, notified of the happening, expressed their astonishment and regret; and were wholly unable to think of any enemy who would care to violate the grave of their ancestor. Hazard Weeden of 598 Angell Street recalls a family legend according to which Ezra Weeden was involved in some very peculiar circumstances, not dishonourable to himself, shortly before the Revolution; but of any modern feud or mystery he is frankly ignorant. Inspector Cunningham has been assigned to the case, and hopes to uncover some valuable clues in the near future.

Dogs Noisy in Pawtuxet

Residents of Pawtuxet were aroused about 3 a.m. today by a phenomenal baying of dogs which seemed to centre near the river just north of Rhodes-on-the-Pawtuxet. The volume and quality of the howling were unusually odd, according to most who heart it; and Fred Lemdin, night watchman at Rhodes, declares it was mixed with something very like the shrieks of a man in mortal terror and agony. A sharp and very brief thunderstorm, which seemed to strike somewhere near the bank of the river, put an end to the disturbance. Strange and unpleasant odours, probably from the oil tanks along the bay, are popularly linked with this incident; and may have had their share in exciting the dogs.

The aspect of Charles Ward now became very haggard and hunted, and all agreed in retrospect that he may have wished at this period to make some statement or confession from which sheer terror withheld him. The morbid listening of his mother in the night brought out the fact that he made frequent sallies abroad under cover of darkness, and most of the more academic alienists unite at present in charging him with the revolting cases of vampirism which the press so sensationally reported about this time, but which have not yet been definitely traced to any known perpetrator. These cases, too recent and celebrated to need detailed mention, involved victims of every age and type and seemed to cluster around two distinct localities; the residential hill and the North End, near the Ward home, and the suburban districts across the Cranston line near Pawtuxet. Both late wayfarers and sleepers with open windows were attacked, and those who lived to tell the tale spoke unanimously of a lean, lithe, leaping monster with burning eyes which fastened its teeth in the throat or upper arm and feasted ravenously.

Dr. Willett, who refuses to date the madness of Charles Ward as far back as even this, is cautious in attempting to explain these horrors. He has, he declares, certain theories of his own; and limits his positive statements to a peculiar kind of negation: 'I will not,' he says, 'state who or what I believe perpetrated these attacks and murders, but I will declare that Charles Ward was innocent of them. I have reason to be sure he was ignorant of the taste of blood, as indeed his continued anaemic decline and increasing pallor prove better than any verbal argument. Ward meddled with terrible things, but he has paid for it, and he was never a monster or a villain. As for now – I don't like to think. A change came, and I'm content to believe that the old Charles Ward died with it. His soul did, anyhow, for that mad flesh that vanished from Waite's hospital had another.'

Willett speaks with authority, for he was often at the Ward home attending Mrs. Ward, whose nerves had begun to snap under the strain. Her nocturnal listening had bred some morbid hallucinations which she confided to the doctor with hesitancy, and which he ridiculed in talking to her, although they made him ponder deeply when alone. These delusions always concerning the faint sounds which she fancied she heard in the attic laboratory and bedroom, and emphasised the occurrence of muffled sighs and sobbings at the most impossible times. Early in July Willett ordered Mrs. Ward to Atlantic City for an indefinite recuperative sojourn, and cautioned both Mr. Ward and the haggard and elusive Charles to write her only cheering letters. It is probably to this enforced and reluctant escape that she owes her life and continued sanity.

2

Not long after his mother's departure, Charles Ward began negotiating for the Pawtuxet bungalow. It was a squalid little wooden edifice with a concrete garage, perched high on the sparsely settled bank of the river slightly above Rhodes, but for some odd reason the youth would have nothing else. He gave the real-estate agencies no peace till one of them secured it for him at an exorbitant price from a somewhat reluctant owner, and as soon as it was vacant he took possession under cover of darkness,, transporting in a great closed van the entire contents of his attic laboratory, including the books both weird and modern which he had borrowed from his study. He had this van loaded in the black small hours, and his father recalls only a drowsy realisation of stifled oaths and stamping feet on the night the goods were taken away. After that Charles moved back to his own old quarters on the third floor, and never haunted the attic again.

To the Pawtuxet bungalow Charles transferred all the secrecy with which he had surrounded his attic realm, save that he now appeared to have two sharers of his mysteries; a villainous-looking Portuguese half-caste from the South Main St. waterfront who acted as a servant, and a thin, scholarly stranger with dark glasses and a stubbly full beard of dyed aspect whose status was evidently that of a colleague. Neighbours vainly tried to engage these odd persons in conversation. The mulatto Gomes spoke very little English, and the bearded man, who gave his name as Dr. Allen, voluntarily followed his example. Ward himself tried to be more affable, but succeeded only in provoking curiousity with his rambling accounts of chemical research. Before long queer tales began to circulate regarding the all-night burning of lights; and somewhat later, after this burning had suddenly ceased, there rose still queerer tales of disproportionate orders of meat from the butcher's and of the muffled shouting, declamation, rhythmic chanting, and screaming supposed to come from some very cellar below the place. Most distinctly the new and strange household was bitterly disliked by the honest bourgeoisie of the vicinity, and it is not remarkable that dark hints were advanced connecting the hated establishment with the current epidemic of vampiristic attacks and murders; especially since the radius of that plague seemed now confined wholly to Pawtuxet and the adjacent streets of Edgewood.

Ward spent most of his time at the bungalow, but slept occasionally at home and was still reckoned a dweller beneath his father's roof. Twice he was absent from the city on week-long trips, whose destinations have not yet been discovered. He grew steadily paler and more emaciated even than before, and lacked some of his former assurance when repeating to Dr. Willett his old, old story of vital research and future revelations. Willett often waylaid him at his father's house, for the elder Ward was deeply worried and perplexed, and wished his son to get as much sound oversight as could be managed in the case of so secretive and independent an adult. The doctor still insists that the youth was sane even as late as this, and adduces many a conversation to prove his point.

About September the vampirism declined, but in the following January almost became involved in serious trouble. For some time the nocturnal arrival and departure of motor trucks at the Pawtuxet bungalow had been commented upon, and at this juncture an unforeseen hitch exposed the nature of at least one item of their contents. In a lonely spot near Hope Valley had occurred one of the frequent sordid waylaying of trucks by "hi-jackers" in quest of liquor shipments, but this time the robbers had been destined to receive the greater shock. For the long cases they seized proved upon opening to contain some exceedingly gruesome things; so gruesome, in fact, that the matter could not be kept quiet amongst the denizens of the underworld. The thieves had hastily buried what they discovered, but when the State Police got wind of the matter a careful search was made. A recently arrived vagrant, under promise of immunity from prosecution on any additional charge, at last consented to guide a party of troopers to the spot; and there was found in that hasty cache a very hideous and shameful thing. It would not be well for the national – or even the international – sense of decorum if the public were ever to know what was uncovered by that awestruck party. There was no mistaking it, even by those far from studious officers; and telegrams to Washington ensued with feverish rapidity.

The cases were addressed to Charles Ward at his Pawtuxet bungalow, and State and Federal officials at once paid him a very forceful and serious call. They found him pallid and worried with his two odd companions, and received from him what seemed to be a valid explanation and evidence of innocence. He had needed certain anatomical specimens as part of a programme of research whose depth and genuineness anyone who had known him in the last decade could prove, and had ordered the required kind and number from agencies which he had thought as reasonably legitimate as such things can be. Of the *identity* of the specimens he had known absolutely nothing, and was properly shocked when the inspectors hinted at the monstrous effect on public sentiment and national dignity which a knowledge of the matter would produce. In this statement he was firmly sustained by his bearded colleague Dr. Allen, whose oddly hollow voice carried even more conviction than his own nervous tones; so that in the end the officials took no action, but carefully set down the New York name and address which Ward gave them a basis for a search which came to nothing. It is only fair to add that the specimens were quickly and quietly restored to their proper places, and that the general public will never know of their blasphemous disturbance.

On February 9, 1928, Dr. Willett received a letter from

Charles Ward which he considers of extraordinary importance, and about which he has frequently quarrelled with Dr. Lyman. Lyman believes that this note contains positive proof of a well-developed case of *dementia praecox*, but Willett on the other hand regards it as the last perfectly sane utterance of the hapless youth. He calls especial attention to the normal character of the penmanship; which though shewing traces of shattered nerves, is nevertheless distinctly Ward's own. The text in full is as follows:

> "100 Prospect St.
> Providence, R.I.,
> February 8, 1928.

Dear Dr. Willett:-

I feel that at last the time has come for me to make the disclosures which I have so long promised you, and for which you have pressed me so often. The patience you have shewn in waiting, and the confidence you have shewn in my mind and integrity, are things I shall never cease to appreciate.

And now that I am ready to speak, I must own with humiliation that no triumph such as I dreamed of can ever by mine. Instead of triumph I have found terror, and my talk with you will not be a boast of victory but a plea for help and advice in saving both myself and the world from a horror beyond all human conception or calculation. You recall what those Fenner letters said of the old raiding party at Pawtuxet. That must all be done again, and quickly. Upon us depends more than can be put into words – all civilisation, all natural law, perhaps even the fate of the solar system and the universe. I have brought to light a monstrous abnormality, but I did it for the sake of knowledge. Now for the sake of all life and Nature you must help me thrust it back into the dark again.

I have left that Pawtuxet place forever, and we must extirpate everything existing there, alive or dead. I shall not go there again, and you must not believe it if you ever hear that I am there. I will tell you why I say this when I see you. I have come home for good, and wish you would call on me at the very first moment that you can spare five or six hours continuously to hear what I have to say. It will take that long – and believe me when I tell you that you never had a more genuine professional duty than this. My life and reason are the very least things which hang in the balance.

I dare not tell my father, for he could not grasp the whole thing. But I have told him of my danger, and he has four men from a detective agency watching the house. I don't know how much good they can do, for they have against them forces which even you could scarcely envisage or acknowledge. So come quickly if you wish to see me alive and hear how you may help to save the cosmos from stark hell.

Any time will do – I shall not be out of the house. Don't telephone ahead, for there is no telling who or what may try to intercept you. And let us pray to whatever gods there be that nothing may prevent this meeting.

In utmost gravity and desperation,

Charles Dexter Ward.

P.S. Shoot Dr. Allen on sight *and dissolve his body in acid. Don't burn it.*"

Dr. Willett received this note about 10:30 a.m., and immediately arranged to spare the whole late afternoon and evening for the momentous talk, letting it extend on into the night as long as might be necessary. He planned to arrive about four o'clock, and through all the intervening hours was so engulfed in every sort of wild speculation that most of his tasks were very mechanically performed. Maniacal as the letter would have sounded to a stranger, Willett had seen too much of Charles Ward's oddities to dismiss it as sheer raving. That something very subtle, ancient, and horrible was hovering about he felt quite sure, and the reference to Dr. Allen could almost be comprehended in view of what Pawtuxet gossip said of Ward's enigmatical colleague. Willett had never seen the man, but had heard much of his aspect and bearing, and could not but wonder what sort of eyes those much-discussed dark glasses might conceal.

Promptly at four Dr. Willett presented himself at the Ward residence, but found to his annoyance that Charles had not adhered to his determination to remain indoors. The guards were there, but said that the young man seemed to have lost part of his timidity. He had that morning done much apparently frightened arguing and protesting over the telephone, one of the detectives said, replying to some unknown voice with phrases such as 'I am very tired and must rest a while', 'I can't receive anyone for some time', 'you'll have to excuse me', 'Please postpone decisive action till we can arrange some sort of compromise', or 'I am very sorry, but I must take a complete vacation from everything; I'll talk with you later.' Then, apparently gaining boldness through meditation, he had slipped out so quietly that no one had seen him depart or knew that he had gone until he returned about one o'clock and entered the house without a word. He had gone upstairs, where a bit of his fear must have surged back; for he was heard to cry out in a highly terrified fashion upon entering his library, afterward trailing off into a kind of choking gasp. When, however, the butler had gone to inquire what the trouble was, he had appeared at the door with a great show of boldness, and had silently gestured the man away in a manner that terrified him unaccountably. Then he had evidently done some rearranging of his shelves, for a great clattering and thumping and creaking ensued; after which he had reappeared and left at once. Willett inquired whether or not any message had been left, but was told that there was no none. The butler seemed queerly disturbed about something in Charles's appearance and manner, and asked solicitously if there was much hope for a cure of his disordered nerves.

For almost two hours Dr. Willett waited vainly in Charles Ward's library, watching the dusty shelves with their wide gaps where books had been removed, and smiling grimly at the panelled overmantel on the north wall, whence a year before the suave features of old Joseph Curwen had looked mildly down. After a time the shadows began to gather, and the sunset cheer gave place to a vague growing terror which flew shadow-like before the night. Mr. Ward finally arrived, and shewed much surprise and anger at his son's absence after all the pains which had been taken to guard him. He had not known of Charles's appointment, and promised to notify Willett when the youth returned. In bidding the doctor goodnight he expressed his utter perplexity at his son's condition, and urged his caller to do all he could to restore the boy to normal poise. Willett was glad to escape from that library, for something frightful and unholy seemed to haunt it; as if the vanished picture had left behind a legacy of evil. He had never liked that picture; and even now, strong-nerved though he was, there lurked a quality in its vacant panel which made him feel an urgent need to get out into the pure air as soon as possible.

The next morning Willett received a message from the senior Ward, saying that Charles was still absent. Mr. Ward mentioned that Dr. Allen had telephoned him to say that Charles would remain at Pawtuxet for some time, and that he must not be disturbed. This was necessary because Allen himself was suddenly called away for an indefinite period, leaving the researches in need of Charles's constant oversight. Charles sent his best wishes, and regretted any bother his abrupt change of plans might have caused. It listening to this message Mr. Ward heard Dr. Allen's voice for the first time, and it seemed to excite some vague and elusive memory which could not be actually placed, but which was disturbing to the point of fearfulness.

Faced by these baffling and contradictory reports, Dr. Willett was frankly at a loss what to do. The frantic earnestness of Charles's note was not to be denied, yet what could one think of its writer's immediate violation of his own expressed policy? Young Ward had written that his delvings had become blasphemous and menacing, that they and his bearded colleague must be extirpated at any cost, and that he himself would never return to their final scene; yet according to latest advices he had forgotten all this and was back in the thick of the mystery. Common sense bade one leave the youth alone with his freakishness, yet some deeper instinct would not permit the impression of that frenzied letter to subside. Willett read it over again, and could not make its essence sound as empty and insane as both its bombastic verbiage and its lack of fulfilment would seem to imply. Its terror was too profound and real, and in conjunction with what the doctor already knew evoked too vivid hints of monstrosities from beyond time and space to permit of any cynical explanation. There were nameless horrors abroad; and no matter how little one might be able to get at them, one ought to stand prepared for any sort of action at any time.

For over a week Dr. Willett pondered on the dilemma which seemed thrust upon him, and became more and more inclined to pay Charles a call at the Pawtuxet bungalow. No friend of the youth had ever ventured to storm this forbidden retreat, and even his father knew of its interior only from such descriptions as he chose to give; but Willett felt that some direct conversation with his patient was necessary. Mr. Ward had been receiving brief and non-committal typed notes from his son, and said that Mrs. Ward in her Atlantic City retirement had had no better word. So at length the doctor resolved to act; and despite a curious sensation inspired by old legends of Joseph Curwen, and by more recent revelations and warnings from Charles Ward, set boldly out for the bungalow on the bluff above the river.

Willett had visited the spot before through sheer curiousity, though of course never entering the house or proclaiming his presence; hence knew exactly the route to take. Driving out Broad Street one early afternoon toward the end of February in his small motor, he thought oddly of the grim party which had taken that selfsame road a hundred and fifty-seven years before on a terrible errand which none might ever comprehend.

The ride through the city's decaying fringe was short, and trim Edgewood and sleepy Pawtuxet presently spread out ahead. Willett turned to the right down Lockwood Street and drove his car as far along that rural road as he could, then alighted and walked north to where the bluff towered above the lovely bends of the river and the sweep of misty downlands beyond. Houses were still few here, and there was no mistaking the isolated bungalow with its concrete garage on a high point of land at his left. Stepping briskly up the neglected gravel walk he rapped at the door with a firm hand, and spoke without a tremor to the evil Portuguese mulatto who opened it to the width of a crack.

He must, he said, see Charles Ward at once on vitally important business. No excuse would be accepted, and a repulse would mean only a full report of the matter to the elder Ward. The mulatto still hesitated, and pushed against the door when Willett attempted to open it; but the doctor merely raised his voice and renewed his demands. Then there came from the dark interior a husky whisper which somehow chilled the hearer through and through though he did not know why he feared it. 'Let him in, Tony,' it said, 'we may as well talk now as ever.' But disturbing as was the whisper, the greater fear was that which immediately followed. The floor creaked and the speaker hove in sight – and the owner of those strange and resonant tones was seen to be no other than Charles Dexter Ward.

The minuteness with which Dr. Willett recalled and recorded his conversation of that afternoon is due to the importance he assigns to this particular period. For at last he concedes a vital change in Charles Dexter Ward's mentality, and believes that the youth now spoke from a brain hopelessly alien to the brain whose growth he had watched for six and twenty years. Controversy with Dr. Lyman has compelled him to be very specific, and he definitely dates the madness of Charles Ward from the time the typewritten notes began to reach his parents. Those notes are not in Ward's normal style; not even in the style of that last frantic letter to Willett. Instead, they are strange and archaic, as if the snapping of the writer's mind had released a flood of tendencies and impressions picked up unconsciously through boyhood antiquarianism. There is an obvious effort to be modern, but the spirit and occasionally the language are those of the past.

The past, too, was evident in Ward's every tone and gesture as he received the doctor in that shadowy bungalow. He bowed, motioned Willett to a seat, and began to speak abruptly in that strange whisper which he sought to explain at the very outset.

'I am grown phthisical,' he began, 'from this cursed river air. You must excuse my speech. I suppose you are come from my father to see what ails me, and I hope you will say nothing to alarm him.'

Willett was studying these scraping tones with extreme care, but studying even more closely the face of the speaker. Something, he felt, was wrong; and he thought of what the family had told him about the fright of that Yorkshire butler one night. He wished it were not so dark, but did not request that the blind be opened. Instead, he merely asked Ward why he had so belied the frantic note of little more than a week before.

'I was coming to that,' the host replied. 'You must know, I am in a very bad state of nerves, and do and say queer things I cannot account for. As I have told you often, I am on the edge of great matters; and the bigness of them has a way of making me light-headed. Any man might well be frighted of what I have found, but I am not to be put off for long. I was a dunce to have that guard and stick at home; for having gone this far, my place is here. I am not well spoke of my prying neighbours, and perhaps I was led by weakness to believe myself what they say of me. There is no evil to any in what I do, so long as I do it rightly. Have the goodness to wait six months, and I'll shew you what will pay your patience well.'

'You may as well know I have a way of learning old matters from things surer than books, and I'll leave you to judge the importance of what I can give to history, philosophy, and the arts by reason of the doors I have access to. My ancestor had all this when those witless peeping Toms came and murdered him. I now have it again, or am coming very imperfectly to have a part of it. This time nothing must happen, and least of all though any idiot fears of my own. Pray forget all I writ you, Sir, and have no fear of this place or any in it. Dr. Allen is a man of fine parts, and I own him an apology for anything ill I have said of him. I wish I had no need to spare him, but there were things he had to do elsewhere. His zeal is equal to mine in all those matters, and I suppose that when I feared the work I feared him too as my greatest helper in it.'

Ward paused, and the doctor hardly knew what to say or think. He felt almost foolish in the face of this calm repudiation of the letter; and yet there clung to him the fact that while the present discourse was strange and alien and indubitably mad, the note itself had been tragic in its naturalness and likeness to the Charles Ward he knew. Willett now tried to turn the talk on early matters, and recall to the youth some past events which would restore a familiar mood; but in this process he obtained only the most grotesque results. It was the same with all the alienists later on. Important sections of Charles Ward's store of mental images, mainly those touching modern times and his own personal life, had been unaccountably expunged; whilst all the massed antiquarianism of his youth had welled up from some profound subconsciousness to engulf the contemporary and the individual. The youth's intimate knowledge of elder things was abnormal and unholy, and he tried his best to hide it. When Willett would mention some favourite object of his boyhood archaistic studies he often shed by pure accident such a light as no normal mortal could conceivably be expected to possess, and the doctor shuddered as the glib allusion glided by.

It was not wholesome to know so much about the way the fat sheriff's wig fell off as he leaned over at the play in Mr. Douglass's Histrionick Academy in King Street on the eleventh of February, 1762, which fell on a Thursday; or about how the actors cut the text of Steele's *Conscious Lover* so badly that one was almost glad the Baptist-ridden legislature closed the theatre a fortnight later. That Thomas Sabin's Boston coach was "damn'd uncomfortable" old letters may well have told; but what healthy antiquarian could recall how the creaking of Epenetus Olney's new signboard (the gaudy crown he set up after he took to calling his tavern the Crown Coffee House) was exactly like the first few notes of the new jazz piece all the radios in Pawtuxet were playing?

Ward, however, would not be quizzed long in this vein. Modern and personal topics he waved aside quite summarily, whilst regarding antique affairs he soon shewed the plainest boredom. What he wished clearly enough was only to satisfy his visitor enough to make him depart without the intention of returning. To this end he offered to shew Willett the entire house, and at once proceeded to lead the doctor through every room from cellar to attic. Willett looked sharply, but noted that the visible books were far too few and trivial to have ever filled the wide gaps on Ward's shelves at home, and that the meagre so-called "laboratory" was the flimsiest sort of a blind. Clearly, there were a library and a laboratory elsewhere; but just where, it was impossible to say. Essentially defeated in his quest for something he could not name, Willett returned to town before evening and told the senior Ward everything which had occurred. They agreed that the youth must be definitely out of his mind, but decided that nothing drastic need be done just then. Above all, Mrs. Ward must be kept in as complete an ignorance as her son's own strange typed notes would permit.

Mr. Ward now determined to call in person upon his son, making it wholly a surprise visit. Dr. Willett took him in his car one evening, guiding him to within sight of the bungalow and waiting patiently for his return. The session was a long one, and the father emerged in a very saddened and perplexed state. His reception had developed much like Willett's, save that Charles had been an excessively long time in appearing after the visitor had forced his way into the hall and sent the Portuguese away with an imperative demand; and in the bearing of the altered son there was no trace of filial affection. The lights had been dim, yet even so the youth had complained that they dazzled him outrageously. He had not spoken out loud at all, averring that his throat was in very poor condition; but in his hoarse whisper there was a quality so vaguely disturbing that Mr. Ward could not banish it from his mind.

Now definitely leagued together to do all they could toward the youth's mental salvation, Mr. Ward and Dr. Willett set about collecting every scrap of data which the case might afford. Pawtuxet gossip was the first item they studied, and this was relatively easy to glean since both had friends in that region. Dr. Willett obtained the most rumours because people talked more frankly to him than to a parent of the central figure, and from all he heard he could tell that young Ward's life had become indeed a strange one. Common tongues would not dissociate his household from the vampirism of the previous summer, while the nocturnal comings and goings of the motor trucks provided their share of dark speculations. Local tradesmen spoke of the queerness of the orders brought them by the evil-looking mulatto, and in particular of the inordinate amounts of mean and fresh blood secured from the two butcher shops in the immediate neighbourhood. For a household of only three, these quantities were quite absurd.

Then there was the matter of the sounds beneath the earth. Reports of these things were harder to point down, but all the vague hints tallied in certain basic essentials. Noises of a ritual nature positively existed, and at times when the bungalow was dark. They might, of course, have come from the known cellar; but rumour insisted that there were deeper and more spreading crypts. Recalling the ancient tales of Joseph Curwen's catacombs, and assuming for granted that the present bungalow had been selected because of its situation on the old Curwen site as revealed in one of another of the documents found behind the picture, Willett and Mr. Ward gave this phase of the gossip much attention; and searched many times without success for the door in the river-bank which old manuscripts mentioned. As to popular opinions of the bungalow's various inhabitants, it was soon plain that the Brava Portuguese was loathed, the bearded and spectacled Dr. Allen feared, and the pallid young scholar disliked to a profound degree. During the last week or two Ward had obviously changed much, abandoning his attempts at affability and speaking only in hoarse but oddly repellent whispers on the few occasions that he ventured forth.

Such were the shreds and fragments gathered here and there; and over these Mr. Ward and Dr. Willett held many long and serious conferences. They strove to exercise deduction, induction, and constructive imagination to their utmost extent; and to correlate every known fact of Charles's later life, including the frantic letter which the doctor now shewed the father, with the meagre documentary evidence available concerning old Joseph Curwen. They would have given much for a glimpse of the papers Charles had found, for very clearly the key to the youth's madness lay in what he had learned of the ancient wizard and his doings.

And yet, after all, it was from no step of Mr. Ward's or Dr. Willett's that the next move in this singular case proceeded. The father and the physician, rebuffed and confused by a shadow too shapeless and intangible to combat, had rested uneasily on their oars while the typed notes of young Ward to his parents grew fewer and fewer. Then came the first of the month with its customary financial adjustments, and the clerks at certain banks began a peculiar shaking of heads and telephoning from one to the other. Officials who knew Charles Ward by sight went down to the bungalow to ask why every cheque of his appearing at this juncture was a clumsy forgery, and were reassured less than they ought to have been when the youth hoarsely explained that he hand had lately been so much affected by a nervous shock as to make normal writing impossible. He could, he said, from no written characters at all except with great difficulty; and could prove it by the fact that he had been forced to type all his recent letters, even those to his father and mother, who would bear out the assertion.

What made the investigators pause in confusion was not this circumstance alone, for that was nothing unprecedented or fundamentally suspicious, nor even the Pawtuxet gossip, of which one or two of them had caught echoes. It was the muddled discourse of the young man which nonplussed them, implying as it did a virtually total loss of memory concerning important monetary matters which he had had at his fingertips only a month or two before. Something was wrong; for despite the apparent coherence and rationality of his speech, there could be no normal reason for this ill-concealed blankness on vital points. Moreover, although none of these men knew Ward well, they could not help observing the change in his language and manner. They had heard he was an antiquarian, but even the most hopeless antiquarians do not make daily use of obsolete phraseology and gestures. Altogether, this combination of hoarseness, palsied hands, bad memory, and altered speech and bearing must represent some disturbance or malady of genuine gravity, which no doubt formed the basis of the prevailing odd rumours; and after their departure the party of officials decided that a talk with the senior Ward was imperative.

So on the sixth of March, 1928, there was a long and serious conference in Mr. Ward's office, after which the utterly bewildered father summoned Dr. Willett in a kind of helpless resignation. Willett looked over the strained and awkward signatures of the cheque, and compared them in his mind with the penmanship of that last frantic note. Certainly, the change was radical and profound, and yet there was something damnably familiar about the new writing. It had crabbed and archaic tendencies of a very curious sort, and seemed to result from a type of stroke utterly different from that which the youth had always used. It was strange – but where had he seen it before? On the whole, it was obvious that Charles was insane. Of that there could be no doubt. And since it appeared unlikely that he could handle his property or continue to deal with the outside world much longer, something must quickly be done toward his oversight and possible cure. It was then that the alienists were called in, Drs. Peck and Waite of Providence and Dr. Lyman of Boston, to whom Mr. Ward and Dr. Willett gave the most exhaustive possible history of the case, and who conferred at length in the now unused library of their young patient, examining what books and papers of his were left in order to gain some further notion of his habitual mental cast. After scanning this material and examining the ominous note to Willett they all agreed that Charles Ward's studies had been enough to unseat or at least to warp any ordinary intellect, and wished most heartily that they could see his more intimate volumes and documents; but this latter they knew they could do, if at all, only after a scene at the bungalow itself. Willett now reviewed the whole case with febrile energy; it being at this time that he obtained the statements of the workmen who had seen Charles find the Curwen documents, and that he collated the incidents of the destroyed newspaper items, looking up the latter at the *Journal* office.

On Thursday, the eighth of March, Drs. Willett, Peck, Lyman, and Waite, accompanied by Mr. Ward, paid the youth their momentous call; making no concealment of their object and questioning the now acknowledged patient with extreme minuteness. Charles, although he was inordinately long in answering the summons and was still redolent of strange and noxious laboratory odours when he did finally make his agitated appearance, proved a far from recalcitrant subject; and admitted freely that his memory and balance had suffered somewhat from close application to abstruse studies. He offered no resistance when his removal to other quarters was insisted upon; and seemed, indeed, to display a high degree of intelligence as apart from mere memory. His conduct would have sent his interviewers away in bafflement had not the persistently archaic trend of his speech and unmistakable replacement of modern by ancient ideas in his consciousness marked him out as one definitely removed from the normal. Of his work he would say no more to the group of doctors than he had formerly said to his family and to Dr. Willett, and his frantic note of the previous month he dismissed as mere nerves and hysteria. He insisted that this shadowy bungalow possessed no library possessed no library or laboratory beyond the visible ones, and waxed abstruse in explaining the absence from the house of such odours as now saturated all his clothing. Neighbourhood gossip he attributed to nothing more than the cheap inventiveness of baffled curiousity. Of the whereabouts of Dr. Allen he said he did not feel at liberty to speak definitely, but assured his inquisitors that the bearded and spectacled man would return when needed. In paying off the stolid Brava who resisted all questioning by the visitors, and in closing the bungalow which still seemed to hold such nighted secrets, Ward shewed no signs of nervousness save a barely noticed tendency to pause as though listening for something very faint. He was apparently animated by a calmly philosophic resignation, as if he removal were the merest transient incident which would cause the least trouble if facilitated and disposed of once and for all. It was clear that he trusted to his obviously unimpaired keenness of absolute mentality to overcome all the embarrassments into which his twisted memory, his lost voice and handwriting, and his secretive and eccentric behaviour had led him. His mother, it was agreed, was not to be told of the change; his father supplying typed notes in his name. Ward was taken to the restfully and picturesquely situated private hospital maintained by Dr. Waite on Conanicut Island in the bay, and subjected to the closest scrutiny and questioning by all the physicians connected with the case. It was then that the physical oddities were noticed; the slackened metabolism, the altered skin, and the disproportionate neural reactions. Dr. Willett was the most perturbed of the various examiners, for he had attended Ward all his life and could appreciate with terrible keenness the extent of his physical disorganisation. Even the familiar olive mark on his hip was gone, while on his chest was a great black mole or cicatrice which had never been there before, and which made Willett wonder whether the youth had ever submitted to any of the *witch markings* reputed to be inflicted at certain unwholesome nocturnal meetings in wild and lonely places. The doctor could not keep his mind off a certain transcribed witch-trial record from Salem which Charles had shewn him in the old non-secretive days, and which read: 'Mr. G. B. on that Nighte putt ye Divell his Marke upon Bridget S., Jonathan A., Simon O., Deliverance W., Joseph C., Susan P., Mehitable C., and Deborah B.' Ward's face, too, troubled him horribly, till at length he suddenly discovered why he was horrified. For above the young man's right eye was something which he had never previously noticed – a small scar or pit precisely like that in the crumbled painting of old Joseph Curwen, and perhaps attesting some hideous ritualistic inoculation to which both had submitted at a certain stage of their occult careers.

While Ward himself was puzzling all the doctors at the hospital a very strict watch was kept on all mail addressed either to him or to Dr. Allen, which Mr. Ward had ordered delivered at the family home. Willett had predicted that very little would be found, since any communications of a vital nature would probably have been exchanged by messenger; but in the latter part of March there did come a letter from Prague for Dr. Allen which gave both the doctor and the father deep thought. It was in a very crabbed and archaic hand; and though clearly not the effort of a foreigner, shewed almost as singular a departure from modern English as the speech of young Ward himself. It read:

"Kleinstrasse 11,
Altstadt, Prague,
11th Feby. 1928.

Brother in Almonsin-Metraton:–

I this day receiv'd yr mention of what came up from the Saltes I sent you. It was wrong, and meanes clearly that ye Headstones had been chang'd when Barnabas gott me the Specimen. It is often so, as you must be sensible of from the Thing you gott from ye Kings Chapell ground in 1769 and what H. gott from Olde Bury'g Point in 1690, that was like to ende him. I gott such a Thing in Aegypt 75 yeares gone, from the which came that Scar ye Boy saw on me here in 1924. As I told you longe ago, do not calle up That which you can not put downe; either from dead Saltes or out of ye Spheres beyond. Have ye Wordes for laying at all times readie, and stopp not to be sure when there is any Doubte of Whom you have. Stones are all chang'd now in Nine groundes out of 10. You are never sure till you question. I this day heard from H., who has had Trouble with the Soldiers. He is like to be sorry Transylvania is pass't from Hungary to Roumania, and wou'd change his Seat if the Castel weren't so fulle of What we Knowe. But of this he hath doubtless writ you. In my next Send'g there will be Somewhat from a Hill tomb from ye East that will delight you greatly. Meanwhile forget not I am desirous of B. F. if you can possibly get him for me. You know G. in Philada. better than I. Have him upp firste if you will, but doe not use him soe hard he will be Difficult, for I must speake to him in ye End.

Yogg-Sothoth Neblod Zin

Simon O.

To Mr. J. C. in Providence."

Mr. Ward and Dr. Willett paused in utter chaos before this apparent bit of unrelieved insanity. Only by degrees did they absorb what it seemed to imply. So the absent Dr. Allen, and not Charles Ward, had come to be the leading spirit at Pawtuxet? That must explain the wild reference and denunciation in the youth's last frantic letter. And what of this addressing of the bearded and spectacled stranger as "Mr. J. C."? There was no escaping the inference, but there are limits to possible monstrosity. Who was "Simon O."; the old man Ward had visited in Prague four years previously? Perhaps, but in the centuries behind there had been another Simon O. – Simon Orne, alias Jedediah, of Salem, who vanished in 1771, *and whose peculiar handwriting Dr. Willett now unmistakably recognised from the photostatic copies of the Orne formulae which Charles had once shown him.* What horrors and mysteries, what contradictions and contraventions of Nature, had come back after a century and a half to harass Old Providence with her clustered spires and domes?

The father and the old physician, virtually at a loss what to do or think, went to see Charles at the hospital and questioned him as delicately as they could about Dr. Allen, about the Prague visit, and about what he had learned of Simon or Jedediah Orne of Salem. To all these enquiries the youth was politely non-committal, merely barking in his hoarse whisper that he had found Dr. Allen to have a remarkable spiritual rapport with certain souls from the past, and that any correspondent the bearded man might have in Prague would probably be similarly gifted. When they left, Mr. Ward and Dr. Willett realised to their chagrin that they had really been the ones under catechism; and that without imparting anything vital himself, the confined youth had adroitly pumped them of everything the Prague letter had contained.

Drs. Peck, Waite, and Lyman were not inclined to attach much importance to the strange correspondence of young Ward's companion; for they knew the tendency of kindred eccentrics and monomaniacs to band together, and believed that Charles or Allen had merely unearthed an expatriated counterpart – perhaps one

121

who had seen Orne's handwriting and copied it in an attempt to pose as the bygone character's reincarnation. Allen himself was perhaps a similar case, and may have persuaded the youth into accepting him as an avatar of the long-dead Curwen. Such things had been known before, and on the same basis the hard-headed doctors disposed of Willett's growing disquiet about Charles Ward's present handwriting, as studied from unpremeditated specimens obtained by various ruses. Willett thought he had placed its odd familiarity at last, and that what it vaguely resembled was the bygone penmanship of old Joseph Curwen himself; but this the other physicians regarded as a phase of imitativeness only to be expected in a mania of this sort, and refused to grant it any importance either favourable or unfavourable. Recognising this prosaic attitude in his colleagues, Willett advised Mr. Ward to keep to himself the letter which arrived for Dr. Allen on the second of April from Rakus, Transylvania, in a handwriting so intensely and fundamentally like that of the Hutchinson cipher that both father and physician paused in awe before breaking the seal. This read as follows:

"Castle Ferenczy
7 March 1928.

Dear C.:–

Hadd a Squad of 20 Militia up to talk about what the Country Folk say. Must digg deeper and have less Hearde. These Roumanians plague me damnably, being officious and particular where you cou'd buy a Magyar off with a Drinke and Food.

Last monthe M. got me ye Sarcophagus of ye Five Sphinxes from ye Acropolis where He whome I call'd up say'd it wou'd be, and I have hadde 3 Talkes with What was therein inhum'd. It will go to S. O. in Prague directly, and thence to you. It is stubborn but you know ye Way with Such.

You shew Wisdom in having lesse about than Before; for there was no Neede to keep the Guards in Shape and eat'g off their Heads, and it made Much to be founde in Case of Trouble, as you too welle knowe. You can now move and worke elsewhere with no Kill'g Trouble if needful, tho' I hope no Thing will soon force you to so Bothersome a Course.

I rejoice that you traffick not so much with Those Outside; for there was ever a Mortall Peril in it, and you are sensible what it did when you ask'd Protection of One not dispos'd to give it.

You excel me in gett'g ye Formulae so another may saye them with Success, but Borellus fancy'd it wou'd be so if just ye right Wordes were hadd. Does ye Boy use 'em often? I regret that he growes squeamish, as I fear'd he wou'd when I hadde him here nigh 15 Monthes, but am sensible you knowe how to deal with him. You can't saye him down with ye Formula, for that will Worke only upon such as ye other Formula hath call'd up from Saltes; but you still have strong Handes and Knife and Pistol, and Graves are not harde to digg, nor Acids loth to burne.

O. sayes you have promis'd him B. F. I must have him after. B. goes to you soone, and may he give you what you wishe of that Darke Thing belowe Memphis. Imploy care in what you calle up, and beware of ye Boy.

It will be ripe in a yeare's time to have up ye Legions from Underneath, and then there are no Boundes to what shal be oures. Have Confidence in what I saye, for you knowe O. and I have hadd these 150 yeares more than you to consulte these Matters in.

Nephreu – Ka nai Hadoth

Edw. H.

For J Curwen, Esq.
Providence."

But if Willett and Mr. Ward refrained from shewing this letter to the alienists, they did not refrain from acting upon it themselves. No amount of learned sophistry could controvert the fact that the strangely bearded and spectacled Dr. Allen, of whom Charles's frantic letter had spoken as such a monstrous menace, was in close and sinister correspondence with two inexplicable creatures whom Ward had visited in his travels and who plainly claimed to be survivals or avatars of Curwen's old Salem colleagues; that he was regarding himself as the reincarnation of Joseph Curwen, and that he entertained − or was at least advised to entertain − murderous designs against a "boy" who could scarcely be other than Charles Ward. There was organised horror afoot; and no matter who had started it, the missing Allen was by this time at the bottom of it. Therefore, thanking heaven that Charles was now safe in the hospital, Mr. Ward lost no time in engaging detectives to learn all they could of the cryptic, bearded doctor; finding whence he had come and what Pawtuxet knew of him, and if possible discovering his present whereabouts. Supplying the men with one of the bungalow keys which Charles yielded up, he urged them to explore Allen's vacant room which had been identified when the patient's belongings had been packed; obtaining what clues they could from any effects he might have left about. Mr. Ward talked with the detectives in his son's old library, and they felt a marked relief when they left it at last; for there seemed to hover about the place a vague aura of evil. Perhaps it was what they had heard of the infamous old wizard whose picture had once stared from the panelled overmantel, and perhaps it was something different and irrelevant;

but in any case they all half sensed an intangible miasma which centred in that carven vestige of an older dwelling and which at times almost rose to the intensity of a material emanation.

CHAPTER FIVE

A Nightmare and a Cataclysm

1

And now swiftly followed that hideous experience which has left its indelible mark of fear on the soul of Marinus Bicknell Willett, and has added a decade to the visible age of one whose youth was even then far behind. Dr. Willett had conferred at length with Mr. Ward, and had come to an agreement with him on several points which both felt the alienists would ridicule. There was, they conceded, a terrible movement alive in the world, whose direct connexion with a necromancy even older than the Salem witchcraft could not be doubted. That at least two living men – and one other of whom they dared not think – were in absolute possession of minds or personalities which had functioned as early as 1690 or before was likewise almost unassailably proved even in the face of all known natural laws. What these horrible creatures – and Charles Ward as well – were doing or trying to do seemed fairly clear from their letters and from every bit of light both old and new which had filtered in upon the case. They were robbing the tombs of all the ages, including those of the world's wisest and greatest men, in the hope of recovering from the bygone ashes some vestige of the consciousness and lore which had once animated and informed them.

A hideous traffic was going on among these nightmare ghouls, whereby illustrious bones were bartered with the calm calculativeness of schoolboys swapping books; and from what was extorted from this centuried dust there was anticipated a power and a wisdom beyond anything which the cosmos had ever seen concentred in one man or group. They had found unholy ways to keep their brains alive, either in the same body or different bodies; and had evidently achieved a way of tapping the consciousness of the dead whom they gathered together. There had, it seems, been some truth in chimerical old Borellus when he wrote of preparing from even the most antique remains certain "Essential Saltes" from which the shade of a long-dead living thing might be raised up. There was a formula for evoking such a shade, and another for putting it down; and it had now been so perfected that it could be taught successfully. One must be careful about evocations, for the markers of old graves are not always accurate.

Willett and Mr. Ward shivered as they passed from conclusion to conclusion. Things – presences or voices of some sort – could be drawn down from unknown places as well as from the grave, and in this process also one must be careful. Joseph Curwen had indubitably evoked many forbidden things, and as for Charles – what might one think of him? What forces "outside the spheres" had reached him from Joseph Curwen's day and turned his mind on forgotten things? He had been led to find certain directions, and he had used them. He had talked with the man of horror in Prague and stayed long with the creature in the mountains of Transylvania. And he must have found the grave of Joseph Curwen at last. That newspaper item and what his mother had heard in the night were too significant to overlook. Then he had summoned something, and it must have come. That mighty voice aloft on Good Friday, and those *different* tones in the locked attic laboratory. What were they like, with their depth and hollowness? Was there not here some awful foreshadowing of the dreaded stranger Dr. Allen with his spectral bass? Yes, *that* was what Mr. Ward had felt with vague horror in his single talk with the man − if man it were − over the telephone!

What hellish consciousness or voice, what morbid shade or presence, had come to answer Charles Ward's secret rites behind that locked door? Those voices heard in argument − "must have it red for three months" − Good God! Was not that just before the vampirism broke out? The rifling of Ezra Weeden's ancient grave, and the cries later at Pawtuxet − whose mind had planned the vengeance and rediscovered the shunned seat of elder blasphemies? And then the bungalow and the bearded stranger, and the gossip, and the fear. The final madness of Charles neither father nor doctor could attempt to explain, but they did feel sure that the mind of Joseph Curwen had come to earth again and was following its ancient morbidities. Was daemoniac possession in truth a possibility? Allen had something to do with it, and the detectives must find out more about one whose existence menaced the young man's life. In the meantime, since the existence of some vast crypt beneath the bungalow seemed virtually beyond dispute, some effort must be made to find it. Willett and Mr. Ward, conscious of the sceptical attitude of the alienists, resolved during their final conference to undertake a joint secret exploration of unparalleled thoroughness; and agreed to meet at the bungalow on the following morning with valises and with certain tools and accessories suited to architectural search and underground exploration.

The morning of April 6th dawned clear, and both

explorers were at the bungalow by ten o'clock. Mr. Ward had the key, and an entry and cursory survey were made. From the disordered condition of Dr. Allen's room it was obvious that the detectives had been there before, and the later searchers hoped that they had found some clue which might prove of value. Of course the main business lay in the cellar; so thither they descended without much delay, again making the circuit which each had vainly made before in the presence of the mad young owner. For a time everything seemed baffling, each inch of the earthen floor and stone walls having so solid and innocuous an aspect that the thought of a yearning aperture was scarcely to be entertained. Willett reflected that since the original cellar was dug without knowledge of any catacombs beneath, the beginning of the passage would represent the strictly modern delving of young Ward and his associates, where they had probed for the ancient vaults whose rumour could have reached them by no wholesome means.

The doctor tried to put himself in Charles's place to see how a delver would be likely to start, but could not gain much inspiration from this method. Then he decided on elimination as a policy, and went carefully over the whole subterranean surface both vertical and horizontal, trying to account for every inch separately. He was soon substantially narrowed down, and at last had nothing left but the small platform before the washtubs, which he tried once before in vain. Now experimenting in every possible way, and exerting a double strength, he finally found that the top did indeed turn and slide horizontally on a corner pivot. Beneath it lay a trim concrete surface with an iron manhole, to which Mr. Ward at once rushed with excited zeal. The cover was not hard to lift, and the father had quite removed it when Willett noticed the queerness of his aspect. He was swaying and nodding dizzily, and in the gust of noxious air which swept up from the black pit beneath the doctor soon recognised ample cause.

In a moment Dr. Willett had his fainting companion on the floor above and was reviving him with cold water. Mr. Ward responded feebly, but it could be seen that the mephitic blast from the crypt had in some way gravely sickened him. Wishing to take no chances, Willett hastened out to Broad Street for a taxicab and had soon dispatched the sufferer home despite his weak-voiced protests; after which he produced an electric torch, covered his nostrils with a band of sterile gauze, and descended once more to peer into the new-found depths. The foul air had now slightly abated, and Willett was able to send a beam of light down the Stygian hold. For about ten feet, he saw, it was a sheer cylindrical drop with concrete walls and an iron ladder; after which the hole appeared to strike a flight of old stone steps which must originally have emerged to earth somewhat southwest of the present building.

Willett freely admits that for a moment the memory of the old Curwen legends kept him from climbing down alone into that malodorous gulf. He could not help thinking of what Like Fenner had reported on that last monstrous night. Then duty asserted itself and he made the plunge, carrying a great valise for the removal of whatever papers might prove of supreme importance. Slowly, as befitted one of his years, he descended the ladder and reached the slimy steps below. This was ancient masonry, his torch told him; and upon the dripping walls he saw the unwholesome moss of centuries. Down, down, ran the steps; not spirally, but in three abrupt turns; and with such narrowness that two men could have passed only with difficulty. He had counted about thirty when a sound reached him very faintly; and after that he did not feel disposed to count any more.

It was a godless sound; one of those low-keyed, insidious outrages of Nature which are not meant to be. To call it a dull wail, a doom-dragged whine, or a hopeless howl of chorused anguish and stricken flesh without mind would be to miss its quintessential loathsomeness and soul-sickening overtones. Was it for this that Ward had seemed to listen on that day he was removed? It was the most shocking thing that Willett had ever heard, and it continued from no determinate point as the doctor reached the bottom of the steps and cast his torchlight around on lofty corridor walls surmounted by Cyclopean vaulting and pierced by numberless black archways. The hall in which he stood was perhaps fourteen feet high in the middle of the vaulting and ten or twelve feet broad. Its pavement was of large chipped flagstone, and its walls and roof were of dressed masonry. Its length he could not imagine, for it stretched ahead indefinitely into the blackness. Of the archways, some had doors of the old six-panelled colonial type, whilst others had none.

Overcoming the dread induced by the smell and the howling, Willett began to explore these archways one by one; finding beyond them rooms with groined stone ceilings, each of medium size and apparently of bizarre used. Most of them had fireplaces, the upper courses of whose chimneys would have formed an interesting study in engineering. Never before or since had he seen such instruments or suggestions of instruments as here loomed up on every hand through the burying dust and cobwebs of a century and a half, in many cases evidently shattered as if by the ancient raiders. For many of the chambers seemed wholly untrodden by modern feet, and must have represented the earliest and most obsolete phases of Joseph Curwen's experimentation. Finally there came a room of obvious modernity, or at least of recent occupancy. There were oil heaters, bookshelves and tables, chairs and cabinets, and a desk piled high with papers of varying antiquity and contemporaneousness. Candlesticks and oil lamps stood about in several places; and finding a match-safe handy, Willett lighted such as were ready for use.

In the fuller gleam it appeared that this apartment was nothing less than the latest study or library of Charles Ward. Of the books the doctor had seen many before, and a good part of the furniture had plainly come from the Prospect Street mansion. Here and there was a piece well known to Willett, and the sense of familiarity became so great that he half forgot the noisomness and the wailing, both of which were plainer here than they had been at the foot of the steps. His first duty, as planned long ahead, was to find and seize any papers which might seem of vital importance; especially those portentous documents found by Charles so long ago behind the picture in Olney Court. As he search he perceived how stupendous a task the final unravelling would be; for file on file was stuffed with papers in curious hands and bearing curious designs, so that months or even years might be needed for a thorough deciphering and editing. Once he found three large packets of letters with Prague and Rakus postmarks, and in writing clearly recognisable as Orne's and Hutchinson's; all of which he took with him as part of the bundle to be removed in his valise.

At last, in a locked mahogany cabinet once gracing the Ward home, Willett found the batch of old Curwen papers; recognising them from the reluctant glimpse Charles had granted him so many years ago. The youth had evidently kept them together very much as they had been when first he found them, since all the titles recalled by the workmen were present except the papers addressed to Orne and Hutchinson, and the cipher with its key.

Willett placed the entire lot in his valise and continued his examination of the files. Since young Ward's immediate condition was the greatest matter at stake, the closest searching was done among the most obviously recent matter; and in this abundance of contemporary manuscript one very baffling oddity was noted. The oddity was the slight amount in Charles's normal writing, which indeed included nothing more recent than two months before. On the other hand, there were literally reams of symbols and formulae, historical notes and philosophical comment, in a crabbed penmanship absolutely identical with the ancient script of Joseph Curwen, though of undeniably modern dating. Plainly, a part of the latter-day programme had been a sedulous imitation of the old wizard's writing, which Charles seemed to have carried to a marvellous state of perfection. Of any third hand which might have been Allen's there was not a trace. If he had indeed come to be the leader, he must have forced young Ward to act as his amanuensis.

In this new material one mystic formula, or rather pair of formulae, recurred so often that Willett had it by heart before he had half finished his quest. It consisted of two parallel columns, the left-hand one surmounted by the archaic symbol called "Dragon's Head" and used in almanacs to indicate the ascending node, and the right-hand one headed by a corresponding sign of "Dragon's Tail" or descending node.

Y'AI 'NG'NGAH,
YOG-SOTHOTH
H'EE-L'GEB
F'AI THRODOG
UAAAH

OGTHROD AI'F
GEB'L-EE'H
YOG-SOTHOTH
'NGAH'NG AI'Y
ZHRO

The appearance of the whole was something like this, and almost unconsciously the doctor realised that the second half was no more than the first written syllabically backward with the exception of the final monosyllables and of the odd name *Yog-Sothoth*, which he had come to recognise under various spellings from other things he had seen in connexion with this horrible matter. The formulae were as follows – *exactly* so, as Willett is abundantly able to testify – and the first one struck an odd note of uncomfortable latent memory in his brain, which he recognised later when reviewing the events of that horrible Good Friday of the previous year. So haunting were these formulae, and so frequently did he come upon them, that before the doctor knew it he was repeating them under his breath. Eventually, however, he felt he had secured all the papers he could digest to advantage for the present; hence resolved to examine no more till he could bring the sceptical alienists en masse for an ampler and more systematic raid. He had still to find the hidden laboratory, so leaving his valise in the lighted room he emerged again into the black noisome corridor whose vaulting echoed ceaseless with that dull and hideous whine.

The next few rooms he tried were all abandoned, or filled only with crumbling boxes and ominous-looking leaden coffins; but impressed him deeply with the magnitude of Joseph Curwen's original operations. He thought of the slaves and seamen who had disappeared, of the graves which had been violated in every part of the world, and of what that final raiding party must have seen; and then he decided it was better not to think any more. Once a great stone staircase mounted at his right, and he deduced that this must have reached to one of the Curwen outbuildings – perhaps the famous stone edifice with the high slit-like windows – provided the steps he had descended had led from the steep-roofed farmhouse.

Suddenly the walls seemed to fall away ahead, and the stench and the wailing grew stronger. Willett saw that he had come upon a vast open space, so great that his torchlight would not carry across it; and as he advanced he encountered occasional stout pillars supporting the arches of the roof.

After a time he reached a circle of pillars grouped like the monoliths of Stonehenge, with a large carved altar on a base of three steps in the centre; and so curious were the carvings on that altar that he approached to study them with his electric light. But when he saw what they were he shrank away shuddering, and did not stop to investigate the dark stains which discoloured the upper surface and had spread down the sides in occasional thin lines. Instead, he found the distant wall and traced it as it swept round in a gigantic circle perforated by occasional black doorways and indented by a myriad of shallow cells with iron gratings and wrist and ankle bonds on chains fastened to the stone of the concave rear masonry. These cells were empty, but still the horrible odour and the dismal moaning continued, more insistent now than ever, and seemingly varied at time by a sort of slippery thumping.

2

From that frightful smell and that uncanny noise Willett's attention could no longer be diverted. Both were plainer and more hideous in the great pillared hall than anywhere else, and carried a vague impression of being far below, even in this dark nether world of subterrene mystery. Before trying any of the black archways for steps leading further down, the doctor cast his beam of light about the stone-flagged floor. It was very loosely paved, and at irregular intervals there would occur a slab curiously pierced by small holes in no definite arrangement, while at one point there lay a very long ladder carelessly flung down. To this ladder, singularly enough, appeared to cling a particularly large amount of the frightful odour which encompassed everything. As he walked slowly about it suddenly occurred to Willett that both the noise and the odour seemed strongest above the oddly pierced slabs, as if they might be crude trap-doors leading down to some still deeper region of horror. Kneeling by one, he worked at it with his hands, and found that with extreme difficulty he could budge it. At his touch the moaning beneath ascended to a louder key, and only with vast trepidation did he persevere in the lifting of the heavy stone. A stench unnameable now rose up from below, and the doctor's head reeled dizzily as he laid back the slab and turned his torch upon the exposed square yard of gaping blackness.

If he had expected a flight of steps to some wide gulf of ultimate abomination, Willett was destined to be disappointed; for amidst that foetor and cracked whining he discerned only the brick-faced top of a cylindrical well perhaps a yard and a half in diameter and devoid of any ladder or other means of descent. As the light shone down, the wailing changed suddenly to a series of horrible yelps; in conjunction with which there came again that sound of blind, futile scrambling and slippery thumping. The explorer trembled, unwilling even to imagine what noxious thing might be lurking in that abyss, but in a moment mustered up the courage to peer over the rough-hewn brink; lying at full length and holding the torch downward at arm's length to see what might lie below. For a second he could distinguish nothing but the slimy, moss-grown brick walls sinking illimitably into that half-tangible miasma of murk and foulness and anguished frenzy; and then he saw that something dark was leaping clumsily and frantically up and down at the bottom of the narrow shaft, which must have been from twenty to twenty-five feet below the stone floor where he lay. The torch shook in his hand, but he looked again to see what manner of living creature might be immured there in the darkness of that unnatural well; left starving by young Ward through all the long month since the doctors had taken him away, and clearly only one of a vast number prisoned in the kindred wells whose pierced stone covers so thickly studded the floor of the great vaulted cavern. Whatever the things were, they could not lie down in their cramped spaces; but must have crouched and whined and waited and feebly leaped all those hideous weeks since their master had abandoned them unheeded.

But Marinus Bicknell Willett was sorry that he looked again; for surgeon and veteran of the dissecting-room though he was, he has not been the same since. It is hard to explain just how a single sight of a tangible object with measurable dimensions could so shake and change a man; and we may only say that there is about certain outlines and entities a power of symbolism and suggestion which acts frightfully on a sensitive thinker's perspective and whispers terrible hints of obscure cosmic relationships and unnameable realities behind the protective illusions of common vision. In that second look Willett saw such an outline or entity, for during the next few instants he was undoubtedly as stark raving mad as any inmate of Dr. Waite's private hospital. He dropped the electric torch from a hand drained of muscular power or nervous coördination, nor heeded the sound of crunching teeth which told of its fate at the bottom of the pit. He screamed and screamed and screamed in a voice whose falsetto panic no acquaintance of his would ever have recognised; and though he could not rise to his feet he crawled and rolled desperately away from the damp pavement where dozens of Tartarean wells poured forth their exhausted whining and yelping to answer his own insane cries. He tore his hands on the rough, loose stones, and many times bruised his head against the frequent pillars, but still he kept on. Then at last he slowly came to himself in the utter blackness and stench, and stopped his ears against the droning wail into which the burst of yelping had subsided. He was drenched with perspiration and without means of producing a light; stricken and unnerved in the abysmal blackness and horror, and crushed with a memory he never could efface. Beneath him dozens of those things still lived, and from one of those shafts the cover was removed. He knew that what he had seen could never climb up the slippery walls, yet shuddered at the thought that some obscure foot-hold might exist.

What the thing was, he would never tell. It was like some of the carvings on the hellish altar, but it was alive. Nature had never made it in this form, for it was too palpably *unfinished*. The deficiencies were of the most surprising sort, and the abnormalities of proportion could not be described. Willett consents only to say that this type of thing must have represented entities which Ward called up from *imperfect salts*, and which he kept for servile or ritualistic purposes. If it had not had a certain significance, its image would not have been carved on that damnable stone. It was not the worst thing depicted on that stone – but Willett never opened the other pits. At the time, the first connected idea in his mind was an idle paragraph from some of the old Curwen data he had digested long before; a phrase used by Simon or Jedediah Orne in that portentous confiscated letter to the bygone sorcerer:

"Certainely, there was Noth'g but ye liveliest Awfulness in that which H. rais'd upp from What he cou'd gather onlie a part of."

Then, horribly supplementing rather than displacing this

image, there came a recollection of those ancient lingering rumours anent the burned, twisted thing found in the fields a week after the Curwen raid. Charles Ward had once told the doctor what old Slocum said of that object; that it was neither thoroughly human, nor wholly allied to any animal which Pawtuxet folk had ever seen or read about.

These words hummed in the doctor's mind as he rocked to and fro, squatting on the nitrous stone floor. He tried to drive them out, and repeated the Lord's Prayer to himself; eventually trailing off into a mnemonic hodge-podge like the modernistic *Waste Land* of Mr. T. S. Eliot, and finally reverting to the oft-repeated dual formula he had lately found in Ward's underground library: '*Y'ai 'ng'ngah, Yog-Sothoth*' and so on till the final underlined '*Zhro*'.

It seemed to soothe him, and he staggered to his feet after a time; lamenting bitterly his fright-lost torch and looking wildly about for any gleam of light in the clutching inkiness of the chilly air. Think he would not; but he strained his eyes in every direction for some faint glint or reflection of the bright illumination he had left in the library. After a while he thought he detected a suspicion of a glow infinitely far away, and toward this he crawled in agonised caution on hands and knees amidst the stench and howling, always feeling ahead lest he collide with the numerous great pillars or stumble into the abominable pit he had uncovered.

Once his shaking fingers touched something which he knew must be the steps leading to the hellish altar, and from this spot he recoiled in loathing. At another time he encountered the pierced slab he had removed, and here his caution became almost pitiful. But he did not come upon the dread aperture after all, nor did anything issue from that aperture to detain him. What had been down there made no sound nor stir. Evidently its crunching of the fallen electric torch had not been good for it. Each time Willett's fingers felt a perforated slab he trembled. His passage over it would sometimes increase the groaning below, but generally it would produce no effect at all, since he moved very noiselessly. Several times during his progress the glow ahead diminished perceptibly, and he realised that the various candles and lamps he had left must be expiring one by one. The thought of being lost in utter darkness without matches amidst this underground world of nightmare labyrinths impelled him to rise to his feet and run, which he could safely do now that he had passed the open pit; for he knew that once the light failed, his only hope of rescue and survival would lie in whatever relief party Mr. Ward might send after missing him for a sufficient period. Presently, however, he emerged from the open space into the narrower corridor and definitely located the glow as coming from a door on his right. In a moment he had reached it and was standing once more in young Ward's secret library, trembling with relief, and watching the sputterings of that last lamp which had brought him to safety.

3

In another moment he was hastily filling the burned-out lamps from an oil supply he had previously noticed, and when the room was bright again he looked about to see if he might find a lantern for further exploration. For racked though he was with horror, his sense of grim purpose was still uppermost; and he was firmly determined to leave no stone unturned in his search for the hideous facts behind Charles Ward's bizarre madness. Failing to find a lantern, he chose the smallest of the lamps to carry; also filling his pockets with candles and matches, and taking with him a gallon can of oil, which he proposed to keep for reserve use in whatever hidden laboratory he might uncover beyond the terrible open space with its unclean altar and nameless covered wells. To traverse that space again would require his utmost fortitude, but he knew it must be done. Fortunately neither the frightful altar nor the opened shaft was near the vast cell-indented wall which bounded the cavern area, and whose black mysterious archways would form the next goals of a logical search.

So Willett went back to that great pillared hall of stench and anguished howling; turning down his lamp to avoid any distant glimpse of the hellish altar, or of the uncovered pit with the pierced stone slab beside it. Most of the black doorways led merely to small chambers, some vacant and some evidently used as storerooms; and in several of the latter he saw some very curious accumulations of various objects. One was packed with rotting and dust-draped bales of spare clothing, and the explorer thrilled when he saw that it was unmistakably the clothing of a century and a half before. In another room he found numerous odds and ends of modern clothing, as if gradual provisions were being made to equip a large body of men. But what he disliked most of all were the huge copper vats which occasionally appeared; these, and the sinister incrustations upon them. He liked them even less than the weirdly figured leaden bowls whose rims retained such obnoxious deposits and around which clung repellent odours perceptible above even the general noisomness of the crypt. When he had completed about half the entire circuit of the wall he found another corridor like that from which he had come, and out of which many doors opened. This he proceeded to investigate; and after entering three rooms of medium size and of no significant contents, he came at last to a large oblong apartment whose business-like tanks and tables, furnaces and modern instruments, occasional books and endless shelves of jars and bottles proclaimed it indeed the long-sought laboratory of Charles Ward – and no doubt of old Joseph Curwen before him.

After lighting the three lamps which he found filled and ready, Dr. Willett examined the place and all the appurtenances with the keenest interest; noting from the relative quantities of various reagents on the shelves that young Ward's dominant concern must have been with some branch of organic chemistry. On the whole, little could be learned from the scientific ensemble, which included a gruesome-looking dissecting-table; so that the room was really rather a disappointment. Among the books was a tattered old copy of Borellus in black-letter, and it was weirdly interesting to note that Ward had underlined the same passage whose marking had so perturbed good Mr. Merritt in Curwen's farmhouse more than a century and half before. That old copy, of course, must have perished along with the rest of Curwen's occult library in the final raid. Three archways opened off the laboratory, and these the doctor proceeded to sample in turn. From his cursory survey he saw that two led merely to small storerooms; but these he canvassed with care, remarking the piles of coffins in various stages of damage and shuddering violently at two or three of the few coffin-plates he could decipher. There was much clothing also stored in these rooms, and several new and tightly nailed boxes which he did not stop to investigate. Most interesting of all, perhaps, were some odd bits which he judged to be fragments of old Joseph Curwen's laboratory appliances. These had suffered damage at the hands of the raiders, but were still partly recognisable as the chemical paraphernalia of the Georgian period.

The third archway led to a very sizeable chamber entirely

lined with shelves and having in the centre a table bearing two lamps. These lamps Willett lighted, and in their brilliant glow studied the endless shelving which surrounded him. Some of the upper levels were wholly vacant, but most of the space was filled with small odd-looking leaden jars of two general types; one tall and without handles like a Grecian lekythos or oil-jug, and the other with a single handle and proportioned like a Phaleron jug. All had metal stoppers, and were covered with peculiar-looking symbols moulded in low relief. In a moment the doctor noticed that these jugs were classified with great rigidity; all the lekythoi being on one side of the room with a large wooden sign reading 'Custodes' above them, and all the Phalerons on the other, correspondingly labelled with a sign reading 'Materia'.

Each of the jars of jugs, except some on the upper shelves that turned out to be vacant, bore a cardboard tag with a number apparently referring to a catalogue; and Willett resolved to look for the latter presently. For the moment, however, he was more interested in the nature of the array as a whole, and experimentally opened several of the lekythoi and Phalerons at random with a view to a rough generalisation. The result was invariable. Both types of jar contained a small quantity of a single kind of substance; a fine dusty powder of very light weight and of many shades of dull, neutral colour. To the colours which formed the only point of variation there was no apparent method of disposal; and no distinction between what occurred in the lekythoi and what occurred in the Phalerons. A bluish-grey powder might be by the side of a pinkish-white one, and any one in a Phaleron might have its exact counterpart in a lekythos. The most individual feature about the powders was their non-adhesiveness. Willett would pour one into his hand, and upon returning it to its jug would find that no residue whatever remained on his palm.

The meaning of the two signs puzzled him, and he wondered why this battery of chemicals was separated so radically from those in glass jars on the shelves of the laboratory proper. "Custodes", "Materia"; that was the Latin for "Guards" and "Materials", respectively – and then there came a flash of memory as to where he had seen that word "Guards" before in connexion with this dreadful mystery. It was, of course, in the recent letter to Dr. Allen purporting to be from old Edwin Hutchinson; and the phrase had read: 'There was no Neede to keep the Guards in Shape and eat'g off their Heads, and it made Much to be founde in Case of Trouble, as you too welle knowe.' What did this signify? But wait – was there not still *another* reference to "guards" in this matter which he had failed wholly to recall when reading the Hutchinson letter? Back in the old non-secretive days Ward had told him of the Eleazar Smith diary recording the spying of Smith and Weeden on the Curwen farm, and in that dreadful chronicle there had been a mention of conversations overheard before the old wizard betook himself wholly beneath the earth. There had been, Smith and Weeden insisted, terrible colloquies wherein figured Curwen, certain captives of his, *and the guards of those captives.* Those guards, according to Hutchinson or his avatar, had "eaten their heads off", so that now Dr. Allen did not keep them *in shape.* And if not *in shape,* how save as the "salts" to which it appears this wizard band was engaged in reducing as many human bodies or skeletons as they could?

So *that* was what these lekythoi contained; the monstrous fruit of unhallowed rites and deeds, presumably won or cowed to such submission as to help, when called up by some hellish incantation, in the defence of their blasphemous master or the questioning of those who were not so willing? Willett shuddered at the thought of what he had been pouring in and out of his hands, and for a moment felt an impulse to flee in panic from that cavern of hideous shelves with their silent and perhaps watching sentinels. Then he thought of the "Materia" – in the myriad Phaleron jugs on the other side of the room. Salts too – and if not the salts of "guards", then the salts of what? God! Could it be possible that here lay the mortal relics of half the titan thinkers of all the ages; snatched by supreme ghouls from crypts where the world thought them safe, and subject to the beck and call of madmen who sought to drain their knowledge for some still wilder end whose ultimate effect would concern, as poor Charles had hinted in his frantic note, "all civilisation, all natural law, perhaps even the fate of the solar system and the universe"? And Marinus Bicknell Willett had sifted their dust through his hands!

Then he noticed a small door at the further end of the room, and calmed himself enough to approach it and examine the crude sign chiselled above. It was only a symbol, but it filled him with vague spiritual dread; for a morbid, dreaming friend of his had once drawn it on paper and told him a few of the things it means in the dark abyss of sleep. It was the sign of Koth, that dreamers see fixed above the archway of a certain black tower standing alone in twilight – and Willett did not like what his friend Randolph Carter had said of its powers. But a moment later he forgot the sign as he recognised a new acrid odour in the stench-filled air. This was a chemical rather than animal smell, and came clearly from the room beyond the door. And it was, unmistakably, the same odour which had saturated Charles Ward's clothing on the day the doctors had taken him away. So it was here that the youth had been interrupted by the final summons? He was wiser that old Joseph Curwen, for he had not resisted. Willett, boldly determined to penetrate every wonder and nightmare this nether realm might contain, seized the small lamp and crossed the threshold. A wave of nameless fright rolled out to meet him, but he yielded to no whim and deferred to no intuition. There was nothing alive here to harm him, and he would not be stayed in his piercing of the eldritch cloud which engulfed his patient.

The room beyond the door was of medium size, and had no furniture save a table, a single chair, and two groups of curious machines with clamps and wheels, which Willett recognised after a moment as mediaeval instruments of torture. On one side of the door stood a rack of savage whips, above which were some shelves bearing empty rows of shallow pedestalled cups of lead shaped like Grecian kylikes. On the other side was the table; with a powerful Argand lamp, a pad and pencil, and two of the stoppered lekythoi from the shelves outside set down at irregular places as if temporarily or in haste. Willett lighted the lamp and looked carefully at the pad, to see what notes Ward might have been jotting down when interrupted; but found nothing more intelligible than the following disjointed fragments in that crabbed Curwen chirography, which shed no light on the case as a whole:

"B. dy'd not. Escap'd into walls and founde Place below."

"Sawe olde V. saye ye Sabaoth and learnt yee Way."

"Rais'd *Yog-Sothoth* thrice and was ye nexte Day deliver'd."

"F. soughte to wipe out all know'g howe to raise Those from Outside."

As the strong Argand blaze lit up the entire chamber the doctor saw that the wall opposite the door, between the two groups of torturing appliances in the corners, was covered with pegs from which hung a set of shapeless-looking robes of a rather dismal yellowish-white. But far more interesting were the two vacant walls, both of which were thickly covered with mystic symbols and formulae roughly chiselled in the smooth dressed stone. The damp floor also bore marks of carving; and with but little difficulty Willett deciphered a huge pentagram in the centre, with a plain circle about three feet wide half way between this and each corner. In one of these four circles, near where a yellowish robe had been flung carelessly down, there stood a shallow kylix of the sort found on the shelves above the whip-rack; and just outside the periphery was one of the Phaleron jugs from the shelves in the other room, its tag numbered 118. This was unstoppered, and proved upon inspection to be empty; but the explorer saw with a shiver that the kylix was not. Within its shallow area, and saved from scattering only by the absence of wind in this sequestered cavern, lay a small amount of a dry, dull-greenish efflorescent powder which must have belonged in the jug; and Willett almost reeled at the implications that came sweeping over him as he correlated little by little the several elements and antecedents of the scene. The whips and the instruments of torture, the dust or salts from the jug of "Materia", the two lekythoi from the "Custodes" shelf, the robes, the formulae on the walls, the notes on the pad, the hints from letters and legends, and the thousand glimpses, doubts, and suppositions which had come to torment the friends and parents of Charles Ward – all these engulfed the doctor in a tidal wave of horror as he looked at that dry greenish powder outspread in the pedestalled leaden kylix on the floor.

With an effort, however, Willett pulled himself together and began studying the formulae chiselled on the walls. From the stained and incrusted letters it was obvious that they were carved in Joseph Curwen's time, and their text was such as to be vaguely familiar to one who had read much Curwen material or delved extensively into the history of magic. One the doctor clearly recognised as what Mrs. Ward heard her son chanting on that ominous Good Friday a year before, and what an authority had told him was a very terrible invocation addressed to secret gods outside the normal spheres. It was not spelled here exactly as Mrs. Ward had set it down from memory, nor yet as the authority had shewn it to him in the forbidden pages of "Eliphas Levi"; but its identity was unmistakable, and such words as *Sabaoth*, *Metraton*, *Almonsin*, and *Zariatnatmik* sent a shudder of fright through the search who had seen and felt so much of cosmic abomination just around the corner.

. This was on the left-hand wall as one entered the room. The right-hand wall was no less thickly inscribed, and Willett felt a start of recognition when he came up the pair of formulae so frequently occurring in the recent notes in the library. They were, roughly speaking, the same; with the ancient symbols of "Dragon's Head" and "Dragon's Tail" heading them as in Ward's scribblings. But the spelling differed quite widely from that of the modern versions, as if old Curwen had had a different way of recording sound, or as if later study had evolved more powerful and perfected variants of the invocations in question. The doctor tried to reconcile the chiselled version with the one which still ran persistently in his head, and found it hard to do. Where the script he had memorised began "Y'ai 'ng'ngah, Yog-Sothoth", this epigraph started out as "Aye, engengah, Yogge-Sothotha"; which to his mind would seriously interfere with the syllabification of the second word.

Ground as the later text was into his consciousness, the discrepancy disturbed him; and he found himself chanting the first of the formulae aloud in an effort to square the sound he conceived

148

with the letters he found carved. Weird and menacing in that abyss of antique blasphemy rang his voice; its accents keyed to a droning sing-song either through the spell of the past and the unknown, or through the hellish example of that dull, godless wail from the pits whose inhuman cadences rose and fell rhythmically in the distance through the stench and the darkness.

"Y'AI 'NG'NGAH,
YOG-SOTHOTH
H'EE-L'GEB
F'AI THRODOG
UAAAH!"

But what was this cold wind which had sprung into life at the very outset of the chant? The lamps were sputtering woefully, and the gloom grew so dense that the letters on the wall nearly faded from sight. There was smoke, too, and an acrid odour which quite drowned out the stench from the far-away wells; an odour like that he had smelt before, yet infinitely stronger and more pungent. He turned from the inscriptions to face the room with its bizarre contents, and saw that the kylix on the floor, in which the ominous efflorescent powder had lain, was giving forth a cloud of thick, greenish-black vapour of surprising volume and opacity. That powder – Great God! it had come from the shelf of "Materia" – what was it doing now, and what had started it? The formula he had been chanting – the first of the pair – Dragon's Head, *ascending node* – Blessed Saviour, could it be ...

The doctor reeled, and through his head raced wildly disjointed scraps from all he had seen, heard, and read of the frightful case of Joseph Curwen and Charles Dexter Ward. "I say to you againe, doe not call up Any that you can not put downe ... Have ye Wordes for laying at all times readie, and stopp not to be sure when there is any Doubte of Whom you have ... Three Talkes with What was therein inhum'd ..." *Mercy of Heaven, what is that shape behind the parting smoke?*

4

Marinus Bicknell Willett has not hope that any part of his tale will be believed except by certain sympathetic friends, hence he has made no attempt to tell it beyond his most intimate circle. Only a few outsiders have ever heard it repeated, and of these the majority laugh and remark that the doctor surely is getting old. He has been advised to take a long vacation and to shun future cases dealing with mental disturbance. But Mr. Ward knows that the veteran physician speaks only a horrible truth. Did not he himself see the noisome aperture in the bungalow cellar? Did not Willett send him home overcome and ill at eleven o'clock that portentous morning? Did he not telephone the doctor in vain that evening, and again the next day, and had he not driven to the bungalow itself on that following noon, finding his friend unconscious but unharmed on one of the beds upstairs? Willett had been breathing stertorously, and opened his eyes slowly when Mr. Ward gave him some brandy fetched from the car. Then he shuddered and screamed, crying out, 'That beard ... those eyes ... God, who are you?' A very strange thing to say to a trim, blue-eyed, clean-shaven gentleman whom he had known from the latter's boyhood.

In the bright noon sunlight the bungalow was unchanged since the previous morning. Willett's clothing bore no disarrangement beyond certain smudges and worn places at the knees, and only a faint acrid odour reminded Mr. Ward of what he had smelt on his son that day he was taken to the hospital. The doctor's flashlight was missing, but his valise was safely there, as empty as when he had brought it. Before indulging in any explanations, and obviously with great moral effort, Willett staggered dizzily down to the cellar and tried the fateful platform before the tubs. It was unyielding. Crossing to where he had left his yet unused tool satchel the day before, he obtained a chisel and began to pry up the stubborn planks one by one. Underneath the smooth concrete was still visible, but of any opening or perforation there was no longer a trace. Nothing yawned this time to sicken the mystified father who had followed the doctor downstairs; only the smooth concrete underneath the planks – no noisome well, no world of subterrene horrors, no secret library, no Curwen papers, no nightmare pits of stench and howling, no laboratory or shelves or chiselled formulae, no ... Dr. Willett turned pale, and clutched at the younger man. 'Yesterday,' he asked softly, 'did you see it here ... and smell it?' And when Mr. Ward, himself transfixed with dread and wonder, found strength to nod an affirmative, the physician gave a sound half a sigh and half a gasp, and nodded in turn. 'Then I will tell you', he said.

So for an hour, in the sunniest room they could find upstairs, the physician whispered his frightful tale to the wondering father. There was nothing to relate beyond the looming up of that form when the greenish-black vapour from the kylix parted, and Willett was too tired to ask himself what had really occurred. There were futile, bewildered head-shakings from both men, and once Mr. Ward ventured a hushed suggestion, 'Do you suppose it would be of any use to dig?' The doctor was silent, for it seemed hardly fitting for any human brain to answer when powers of unknown spheres had so vitally encroached on this side of the Great Abyss. Again Mr. Ward asked, 'But where did it go? It brought you here, you know, and it sealed up the hole somehow.' And Willett again let silence answer for him.

But after all, this was not the final phase of the matter. Reaching for his handkerchief before rising to leave, Dr. Willett's fingers closed upon a piece of paper in his pocket which had not been there before, and which was companioned by the candles and matches he had seized in the vanished vault. It was a common sheet, torn obviously from the cheap pad in that fabulous room of horror somewhere underground, and the writing upon it was that of an ordinary lead pencil – doubtless the one which had lain beside the pad. It was folded very carelessly, and beyond the faint acrid scent of the cryptic chamber bore no print or mark of any world but this. But in the text itself it did indeed reek with wonder; for here was no script of any wholesome age, but the laboured strokes of mediaeval darkness, scarcely legible to the laymen who now strained over it, yet having combinations of symbols which seemed vaguely familiar.

The briefly scrawled message was this, and its mystery lent purpose to the shaken pair, who forthwith walked steadily out to the Ward car and gave orders to be driven first to a quiet dining place and then to the John Hay Library on the hill.

At the library it was easy to find good manuals of palaeography, and over these the two men puzzled till the lights of evening shone out from the great chandelier. In the end they found what was needed. The letters were indeed no fantastic invention, but the normal script of a very dark period. They were the pointed Saxon minuscules of the eighth or ninth century A.D., and brought with them memories of an uncouth time when under a fresh Christian veneer ancient faiths and ancient rites stirred stealthily, and the pale moon of Britain looked sometimes on strange deeds in the Roman ruins of Caerleon and Hexham, and by the towers along Hadrian's crumbling wall. The words were in such Latin as a barbarous age might remember − '*Corvinus necandus est. Cadaver aq(ua) forti dissolvendum, nec aliq(ui)d retinendum. Tace ut potes.*' − which may roughly be translated, "Curwen must be killed. The body must be dissolved in aqua fortis, nor must anything be retained. Keep silence as best you are able."

Willett and Mr. Ward were mute and baffled. They had met the unknown, and found that they lacked emotions to respond to it as they vaguely believed they ought. With Willett, especially, the capacity for receiving fresh impressions of awe was well-nigh exhausted; and both men sat still and helpless till the closing of the library forced them to leave. Then they drove listlessly to the Ward mansion in Prospect Street, and talked to no purpose into the night. The doctor rested toward morning, but did not go home. And he was still there Sunday noon when a telephone message came from the detectives who had been assigned to look up Dr. Allen.

Mr. Ward, who was pacing nervously about in a dressing-gown, answered the call in person; and told the men to come up early the next day when he heard their report was almost ready. Both Willett and he were glad that this phase of the matter was taking form, for whatever the origin of the strange minuscule message, it seemed certain the "Curwen" who must be destroyed could be no other than the bearded and spectacled stranger. Charles had feared this man, and had said in the frantic note that he must be killed and dissolved in acid. Allen, moreover, had been receiving letters from the strange wizards in Europe under the name of Curwen, and palpably regarded himself as an avatar of the bygone necromancer. And now from a fresh and unknown source had come a message saying that "Curwen" must be killed and dissolved in acid. The linkage was too unmistakable to be factitious; and besides, was not Allen planning to murder young Ward upon the advice of the creature called Hutchinson? Of course, the letter they had seen had never reached the bearded stranger; but from its text they could see that Allen had already formed plans for dealing with the youth if he grew too "squeamish". Without doubt, Allen must be apprehended; and even if the most drastic directions were not carried out, he must be placed where he could inflict no harm upon Charles Ward.

That afternoon, hoping against hope to extract some gleam of information anent the inmost mysteries from the only available one capable of giving it, the father and the doctor went down the bay and called on young Charles at the hospital. Simply and gravely Willett told him all he had found, and noticed how pale he turned as each description made certain the truth of the discovery. The physician employed as much dramatic effect as he could, and watched for a wincing on Charles's part when he approached the matter of the covered pits and the nameless hybrids within. But Ward did not wince. Willett paused, and his voice grew indignant as he spoke of how the things were starving. He taxed the youth with shocking inhumanity, and shivered when only a sardonic laugh came in reply. For Charles, having dropped as useless his pretence that the crypt did not exist, seemed to see some ghastly jest in this affair; and chucked hoarsely at something which amused him. Then he whispered, in accents doubly terrible because of the cracked voice he used, 'Damn 'em, they *do* eat, but they *don't need to!* That's the rare part! A month, you say, without food? Lud, Sir, you be modest! D'ye know, that was the joke on poor old Whipple with his virtuous bluster! Kill everything off, would he? Why, damme, he was half-deaf with noise from Outside and never saw or heard aught from the wells! He never dreamed they were there at all! Devil take ye, *those cursed things have been howling down there ever since Curwen was done for a hundred and fifty-seven years gone!*'

But no more than this could Willett get from the youth. Horrified, yet almost convinced against his will, he went on with his tale in the hope that some incident might startle his auditor out of the mad composure he maintained. Looking at the youth's face, the doctor could not but feel a kind of terror at the changes which recent months had wrought. Truly, the boy had drawn down nameless horrors from the skies. When the room with the formulae and the greenish dust was mentioned, Charles shewed his first sign of animation. A quizzical look overspread his face as he heard what Willett had read on the pad, and he ventured the mild statement that those notes were old ones, of no possible significance to anyone not deeply initiated in the history of magic. But, he added, 'had you but known the words to bring up that which I had out in the cup, you had not been here to tell me this. 'Twas Number 118, and I conceive you would have shook had you looked it up in my list in t'other room. 'Twas never raised by me, but I meant to have it up that day you came to invite me hither.'

Then Willett told of the formula he had spoken and of the

greenish-black smoke which had arisen; and as he did so he saw true fear dawn for the first time on Charles Ward's face. 'It *came*, and you be here alive?' As Ward croaked the words his voice seemed almost to burst free of its trammels and sink to cavernous abysses of uncanny resonance. Willett, gifted with a flash of inspiration, believed he saw the situation, and wove into his reply a caution from a letter he remembered. 'No. 118, you say? But don't forget that *stones are all changed now in nine grounds out of ten. You are never sure till you question!* 'And then, without warning, he drew forth the minuscule message and flashed it before the patient's eyes. He could have wished no stronger result, for Charles Ward fainted forthwith.

All this conversation, of course, had been conducted with the greatest secrecy lest the resident alienists accuse the father and the physician of encouraging a madman in his delusions. Unaided, too, Dr. Willett and Mr. Ward picked up the stricken youth and placed him on the couch. In reviving, the patient mumbled many times of some word which he must get to Orne and Hutchinson at once; so when his consciousness seemed fully back the doctor told him that of those strange creatures at least one was his bitter enemy, and had given Dr. Allen advice for his assassination. This revelation produced no visible effect, and before it was made the visitors could see that their host had already the look of a hunted man. After that he would converse no more, so Willett and the father departed presently; leaving behind a caution against the bearded Allen, to which the youth only replied that this individual was very safely taken care of, and could do no one any harm even if he wished. This was said with an almost evil chuckle very painful to hear. They did not worry about any communications Charles might indite to that monstrous pair in Europe, since they knew that the hospital authorities seized all outgoing mail for censorship and would pass no wild or outré-looking missive.

There is, however, a curious sequel to the matter of Orne and Hutchinson, if such indeed the exiled wizards were. Moved by some vague presentiment amidst the horrors of that period, Willett arranged with an international press-cutting bureau for accounts of notable current crimes and accidents in Prague and in eastern Transylvania; and after six months believed that he had found two very significant things amongst the multifarious items he received and had translated. One was the total wrecking of a house by night in the oldest quarter of Prague, and the disappearance of the evil old man called Josef Nadek, who had dwelt in it alone ever since anyone could remember. The other was a titan explosion in the Transylvanian mountains east of Rakus, and the utter extirpation with all its inmates of the ill-regarded Castle Ferenczy, whose master was so badly spoken of by peasants and soldiery alike that he would shortly have been summoned to Bucharest for serious questioning had not this incident cut off a career already so long as to antedate all common memory. Willett maintains that the hand which wrote those minuscules was able to wield stronger weapons as well; and that while Curwen was left to him to dispose of, the writer felt able to find and deal with Orne and Hutchinson itself. If what their fate may have been the doctor strives sedulously not to think.

5

The following morning Dr. Willett hastened to the Ward home to be present when the detectives arrived. Allen's destruction or imprisonment – or Curwen's if one might regard the tacit claim to reincarnation as valid – he felt must be accomplished at any cost, and he communicated this conviction to Mr. Ward as they sat waiting for the men to come. They were downstairs this time, for the upper parts of the house were beginning to be shunned because of a particular nauseousness which hung indefinitely about; a nauseousness which the older servants connected with some curse left by the vanished Curwen portrait.

At nine o'clock the three detectives presented themselves and immediately delivered all that they had to say. They had not, regrettably enough, located the Brava Tony Gomes as they had wished, nor had they found the least trace of Dr. Allen's source or present whereabouts; but they had managed to unearth a considerable number of local impressions and facts concerning the reticent stranger. Allen had struck Pawtuxet people as a vaguely unnatural being, and there was a universal belief that his thick sandy beard was either dyed or false – a belief conclusively upheld by the finding of such a false beard, together with a pair of dark glasses, in his room at the fateful bungalow. His voice, Mr. Ward could well testify from his one telephone conversation, had a depth and hollowness that could not be forgotten; and his glanced seemed malign even through his smoked and horn-rimmed glasses. One shopkeeper, in the course of negotiations, had seen a specimen of his handwriting and declared it was very queer and crabbed; this being confirmed by pencilled notes of no clear meaning found in his room and identified by the merchant. In connexion with the vampirism rumours of the preceding summer, a majority of the gossips believed that Allen rather than Ward was the actual vampire. Statements were also obtained from the officials who had visited the bungalow after the unpleasant incident of the motor truck robbery. They had felt less of the sinister in Dr. Allen, but had recognised him as the dominant figure in the queer shadowy cottage. The place had been too dark for them to observe him clearly, but they would know him again if they saw him. His beard had looked odd, and they thought he had some slight scar above his dark spectacled right eye. As for the detectives' search of Allen's room, it yielded nothing definite save the beard and glasses, and several pencilled notes in a crabbed writing which Willett at once saw was identical with that shared by the old Curwen manuscripts and by the voluminous recent notes of young Ward found in the vanished catacombs of horror.

Dr. Willett and Mr. Ward caught something of a profound, subtle, and insidious cosmic fear from this data as it was gradually unfolded, and almost trembled in following up the vague, mad thought which had simultaneously reached their minds. The false beard and glasses – the crabbed Curwen penmanship – the old portrait and its tiny scar – *and the altered youth in the hospital with such a scar* – that deep, hollow voice on the telephone – was it not of this that Mr. Ward was reminded when his son barked forth those pitiable tones to which he now claimed to be reduced? Who had ever seen Charles and Allen together? Yes, the officials had once, but who later on? Was it not when Allen left that Charles suddenly lost his growing fright and began to live wholly at the bungalow? Curwen – Allen – Ward – in what blasphemous and abominable fusion had two ages and two persons become involved? That damnable resemblance of the picture to Charles – had it not used to stare and stare, and follow the boy around the room with its eyes? Why, too, did both Allen and Charles copy Joseph Curwen's handwriting, even when alone and off guard? And then the frightful work of those people – the lost crypt of horrors that had aged the doctor overnight; the starving monsters in the noisome pits; the awful formula which had yielded such nameless results; the message in minuscules found in Willett's pocket; the papers and the letters and all the talk of graves and "salts" and discoveries – whither did everything lead? In the end Mr. Ward did the most sensible thing. Steeling himself against any realisation of why he did it, he gave the detectives an article to be shewn to such Pawtuxet shopkeepers as had seen the portentous Dr. Allen. That article was a photograph of his luckless son, on which he now carefully drew in ink the pair of heavy glasses and the black pointed beard which the men had brought from Allen's room.

For two hours he waited with the doctor in the oppressive house where fear and miasma were slowly gathering as the empty panel in the upstairs library leered and leered and leered. Then the men returned. Yes. *The altered photograph was a very passable likeness of Dr. Allen.* Mr. Ward turned pale, and Willett wiped a suddenly dampened brow with his handkerchief. Allen – Ward – Curwen – it was becoming too hideous for coherent thought. What had the boy called out of the void, and what had it done to him? What, really, had happened from first to last? Who was this Allen who sought to kill Charles as too "squeamish", and why had his destined victim said in the postscript to that frantic letter that he must be so completely obliterated in acid? Why, too, had the minuscule message, of whose origin no one dared think, said that "Curwen" must be likewise obliterated? What was the *change*, and when had the final stage occurred? That day when his frantic note was received – he had been nervous all the morning, then there was an alteration. He had slipped out unseen and swaggered boldly in past the men hired to guard him. That was the time, when he was out. But no – had he not cried out in terror as he entered his study – this very room? What had he found there? Or wait – *what had found him?* That simulacrum which brushed boldly in without having been seen to go

— was that an alien shadow and a horror forcing itself upon a trembling figure which had never gone out at all? Had not the butler spoken of queer noises?

Willett rang for the man and asked him some low-toned questions. It had, surely enough, been a bad business. There had been noises – a cry, a gasp, a choking, and a sort of clattering or creaking or thumping, or all of these. And Mr. Charles was not the same when he stalked out without a word. The butler shivered as he spoke, and sniffed at the heavy air that blew down from some open window upstairs. Terror had settled definitely upon the house, and only the business-like detectives failed to imbibe a full measure of it. Even they were restless, for this case had held vague elements in the background which pleased them not at all. Dr. Willett was thinking deeply and rapidly, and his thoughts were terrible ones. Now and then he would almost break into muttering as he ran over in his head a new, appalling, and increasingly conclusive chain of nightmare happenings.

Then Mr. Ward made a sign that the conference was over, and everyone save him and the doctor left the room. It was noon now, but shadows as of coming night seemed to engulf the phantom-haunted mansion. Willett began talking very seriously to his host, and urged that he leave a great deal of the future investigation to him. There would be, he predicted, certain obnoxious elements which a friend could bear better than a relative. As family physician he must have a free hand, and the first thing he required was a period alone and undisturbed in the abandoned library upstairs, where the ancient overmantel had gathered about itself an aura of noisome horror more intense than when Joseph Curwen's features themselves glanced slyly down from the painted panel.

Mr. Ward, dazed by the flood of grotesque morbidities and unthinkably maddening suggestions that poured in upon him from every side, could only acquiesce; and half an hour later the doctor was locked in the shunned room with the panelling from Olney Court. The father, listening outside, heard fumbling sounds of moving and rummaging as the moments passed; and finally a wrench and a creak, as if a tight cupboard door were being opened. Then there was a muffled cry, a kind of snorting choke, and a hasty slamming of whatever had been opened. Almost at once the key rattled and Willett appeared in the hall, haggard and ghastly, and demanding wood for the real fireplace on the south wall of the room. The furnace was not enough, he said; and the electric log had little practical use. Longing yet not daring to ask questions, Mr. Ward gave the requisite orders and a man brought some stout pine logs, shuddering as he entered the tainted air of the library to place them in the grate. Willett meanwhile had gone up to the dismantled laboratory and brought down a few odds and ends not included in the moving of the July before. They were in a covered basket, and Mr. Ward never saw what they were.

Then the doctor locked himself in the library once more, and by the clouds of smoke which rolled down past the windows from the chimney it was known that he had lighted the fire. Later, after a great rustling of newspapers, that odd wrench and creaking were heard again; followed by a thumping which none of the eavesdroppers liked. Thereafter two suppressed cries of Willett's were heard, and hard upon these came a swishing rustle of indefinable hatefulness. Finally the smoke that the wind beat down from the chimney grew very dark and acrid, and everyone wished that the weather had spared them this choking and venomous inundation of peculiar fumes. Mr. Ward's head reeled, and the servants all clustered together in a knot to watch the horrible black smoke swoop down. After an age of waiting the vapours seemed to lighted, and half-formless sounds of scraping, sweeping, and other minor operations were heard behind the bolted door. And at last, after the slamming of some cupboard within, Willett made his appearance – sad, pale, and haggard, and bearing the cloth-draped basket he had taken from the upstairs laboratory. He had left the window open, and into that once accursed room was pouring a wealth of pure, wholesome air to mix with a queer new smell of disinfectants. The ancient overmantel still lingered; but it seemed robbed of malignity now, and rose as calm and stately in its white panelling as if it had never borne the picture of Joseph Curwen. Night was coming on, yet this time its shadows held no latent fright, but only a gentle melancholy. Of what he had done the doctor would never speak. To Mr. Ward he said, 'I can answer no questions, but I will say that there are different kinds of magic. I have made a great purgation, and those in this house will sleep the better for it.'

6

That Dr. Willett's "purgation" had been an ordeal almost as nerve-racking in its way as his hideous wandering in the vanished crypt is shewn by the fact that the elderly physician gave out completely as soon as he reached home that evening. For three days he rested constantly in his room, though servants later muttered something about having heard him after midnight on Wednesday, when the outer door softly opened and closed with phenomenal softness. Servants' imaginations, fortunately, are limited, else comment might have been excited by an item in Thursday's *Evening Bulletin* which ran as follows:

North End Ghouls Again Active

After a lull of ten months since the dastardly vandalism in the Weeden lot at the North Burial Ground, a nocturnal prowler was glimpsed early this morning in the same cemetery by Robert Hart, the night watchman. Happening to glance for a moment from his shelter at about 2 a.m., Hart observed the glow of a lantern or pocket torch not far to the northwest, and upon opening the door detected the figure of a man with a trowel very plainly silhouetted against a nearby electric light. At once starting in pursuit, he saw the figure dart hurriedly toward the main entrance, gaining the street and losing himself among the shadows before approach or capture was possible.

Like the first of the ghouls active during the past year, this intruder had done no real damage before detection. A vacant part of the Ward lot shewed signs of a little superficial digging, but nothing even nearly the size of a grave had been attempted, and no previous grave had been disturbed.

Hart, who cannot describe the prowler except as a small man probably having a full beard, inclines to the view that all three of the digging incidents have a common source; but police from the Second Station think otherwise on account of the savage nature of teh second incident, where an ancient coffin was removed and its headstone violently shattered.

The first of the incidents, in which it is thought an attempt to bury something was frustrated, occurred a year ago last March, and has been attributed to bootleggers seeking a cache. It is possible, says Sergt. Riley, that this third affair is of similar nature. Officers at the Second Station are taking especial pains to capture the gang of miscreants responsible for these repeated outrages.

All day Thursday Dr. Willett rested as if recuperating from

something past or nerving himself for something to come. In the evening he wrote a note to Mr. Ward, which was delivered the next morning and which caused the half-dazed parent to ponder long and deeply. Mr. Ward had not been able to go down to business since the shock of Monday with its baffling reports and its sinister "purgation", but he found something calming about the doctor's letter in spite of the despair it seemed to promise and the fresh mysteries it seemed to evoke.

> "10 Barnes St.,
> Providence, R. I.,
> April 12, 1928.

Dear Theodore:–

I feel that I must say a word to you before doing what I am going to do tomorrow. It will conclude the terrible business we have been going through (for I feel that no spade is ever likely to reach that monstrous place we know of), but I'm afraid it won't set your mind at rest unless I expressly assure you how very conclusive it is.

You have known me ever since you were a small boy, so I think you will not distrust me when I hint that some matters are best left undecided and unexplored. It is better that you attempt no further speculation as to Charles's case, and almost imperative that you tell his mother nothing more than she already suspects. When I call on you tomorrow Charles will have escaped. That is all which need remain in anyone's mind. He was mad, and he escaped. You can tell his mother gently and gradually about the mad part when you stop sending the typed notes in his name. I'd advise you to join her in Atlantic City and take a rest yourself. God knows you need one after this shock, as I do myself. I am going South for a while to calm down and brace up.

So don't ask me any questions when I call. It may be that something will go wrong, but I'll tell you if it does. I don't think it will. There will be nothing more to worry about, for Charles will be very, very safe. He is now – safer than you dream. You need hold no fears about Allen, and who or what he is. He forms as much a part of the past as Joseph Curwen's picture, and when I ring your doorbell you may feel certain that there is no such person. And what wrote that minuscule message will never trouble you or yours.

But you must steel yourself to melancholy, and prepare your wife to do the same. I must tell you frankly that Charles's escape will not mean his restoration to you. He has been afflicted with a peculiar disease, as you must realise from the subtle physical as well as mental changes in him, and you must not hope to see him again. Have only this consolation – that he was never a fiend or even truly a madman, but only an eager, studious, and curious boy whose love of mystery and of the past was his undoing. He stumbled on things no mortal ought ever to know, and reached back through the years as no one ever should reach; and something came out of those years to engulf him.

And now comes the matter in which I must ask you to trust me most of all. For there will be, indeed, no uncertainty about Charles's fate. In about a year, say, you can if you wish devise a suitable account of the end; for the boy will be no more. You can put up a stone in your lot at the North Burial Ground exactly ten feet west of your father's and facing the same way, and that will mark the true resting-place of your son. Nor need you fear that it will mark any abnormality or changeling. The ashes in that grave will be those of your own unaltered bone and sinew – of the real Charles Dexter Ward whose mind you watched from infancy – the real Charles with the olive-mark on his hip and without the black witch-mark on his chest or the pit on his forehead. The Charles who never did actual evil, and who will have paid with his life for his "squeamishness".

That is all. Charles will have escaped, and a year from now you can put up his stone. Do not question me tomorrow. And believe that the honour of your ancient family remains untainted now, as it has been at all times in the past.

With profoundest sympathy, and exhortations to fortitude, calmness, and resignation, I am ever

Sincerely your friend,

Marinus B. Willett. "

So on the morning of Friday, April 13, 1928, Marinus Bicknell Willett visited the room of Charles Dexter Ward at Dr. Waite's private hospital on Conanicut Island. The youth, though making no attempt to evade his caller, was in a sullen mood; and seemed disinclined to open the conversation which Willett obviously desired. The doctor's discovery of the crypt and his monstrous experience therein had of course created a new source of embarrassment, so that both hesitated perceptibly after the interchange of a few strained formalities. Then a new element of constraint crept in, as Ward seemed to read behind the doctor's mask-like face a terrible purpose which had never been there before. The patient quailed, conscious that since the last visit there had been a change whereby the solicitous family physician had given place to the ruthless and implacable avenger.

Ward actually turned pale, and the doctor was the first to speak. 'More,' he said, 'has been found out, and I must warn you fairly that a reckoning is due.'

'Digging again, and coming upon more poor starving

167

pets?' was the ironic reply. It was evident that the youth meant to show bravado to the last.

'No,' Willett slowly rejoined, 'this time I did not have to dig. We have had men looking up Dr. Allen, and they found the false beard and spectacles in the bungalow.'

'Excellent,' commented the disquieted host in an effort to be wittily insulting, 'and I trust they proved more becoming than the beard and glasses you now have on!'

'They would become you very well,' came the even and studied response, *'as indeed they seem to have done.'*

As Willett said this, it almost seemed as though a cloud passed over the sun; though there was no change in the shadows on the floor. Then Ward ventured:

'And is this what asks so hotly for a reckoning? Suppose a man does find it now and then useful to be twofold?'

'No', said Willett gravely, 'again you are wrong. It is no business of mine if any man seeks duality; *provided he has any right to exist at all, and provided he does not destroy what called him out of space.'*

Ward now started violently. 'Well, Sir, what *have* ye found, and what d'ye want of me?'

The doctor let a little time elapse before replying, as if choosing his words for an effective answer.

'I have found', he finally intoned, 'something in a cupboard behind an ancient overmantel where a picture once was, and I have burned it and buried the ashes where the grave of Charles Dexter Ward ought to be.'

The madman choked and sprang from the chair in which he had been sitting:

'Damn ye, who did ye tell – and who'll believe it was he after these two full months, with me alive? What d'ye mean to do?'

Willett, though a small man, actually took on a kind of judicial majesty as he calmed the patient with a gesture.

'I have told no one. This is no common case – it is a madness out of time and a horror from beyond the spheres which no police or lawyers or courts or alienists could ever fathom or grapple with. Thank God some chance has left inside me the spark of imagination, that I might not go astray in thinking out this thing. *You cannot deceive me, Joseph Curwen, for I know that your accursed magic is true!'*

'I know how you wove the spell that brooded outside the years and fastened on your double and descendant; I know how you drew him into the past and got him to raise you up from your detestable grave; I know how he kept you hidden in his laboratory while you studied modern things and roved abroad as a vampire by night, and how you later shewed yourself in beard and glasses that no one might wonder at your godless likeness to him; I know what you resolved to do when he balked at your monstrous rifling of the world's tombs, *and at what you planned afterward* , and I know how you did it.'

'You left off your beard and glasses and fooled the guards around the house. They thought it was he who went in, and they thought it was he who came out when you had strangled and hidden him. But you hadn't reckoned on the different contents of two minds. You were a fool, Joseph Curwen, to fancy that a mere visual identity would be enough. Why didn't you think of the speech and the voice and the handwriting? It hasn't worked, you see, after all. You know better than I who or what wrote that message in minuscules, but I will warn you it was not written in vain. There are abominations and blasphemies which must be stamped out, and I believe that the writer of those words will attend to Orne and Hutchinson. One of those creatures wrote you once, "do not call up any that you can not put down". You were undone once before, perhaps in that very way, and it may be that your own evil magic will undo you all again. Curwen, a man can't tamper with Nature beyond certain limits, and every horror you have woven will rise up to wipe you out.'

But here the doctor was cut short by a convulsive cry from the creature before him. Hopelessly at bay, weaponless, and knowing that any show of physical violence would bring a score of attendants to the doctor's rescue, Joseph Curwen had recourse to his one ancient ally, and began a series of cabbalistic motions with his forefingers as his deep, hollow voice, now unconcealed by feigned hoarseness, bellowed out the opening words of a terrible formula.

'PER ADONAI ELOIM, ADONAI JEHOVA, ADONAI SABAOTH, METRATON...'

But Willett was too quick for him. Even as the dogs in the yard outside began to howl, and even as a chill wind sprang suddenly up from the bay, the doctor commenced the solemn and measured intonation of that which he had meant all along to recite. An eye for an eye – magic for magic – let the outcome shew how well the lesson of the abyss had been learned! So in a clear voice Marinus Bicknell Willett began the *second* of that pair of formulae whose first had raised the writer of those minuscules – the cryptic invocation whose heading was the Dragon's Tail, sign of the *descending node* –

"OGTHROD AI'F
GEB'L-EE'H
YOG-SOTHOTH
'NGAH'NG AI'Y
ZHRO!"

At the very first word from Willett's mouth the previously commenced formula of the patient stopped short. Unable to speak, the monster made wild motions with his arms until they too were arrested. When the awful name of *Yog-Sothoth* was uttered, the hideous change began. It was not merely a *dissolution*, but rather a *transformation* or *recapitulation*; and Willett shut his eyes lest he faint before the rest of the incantation could be pronounced.

But he did not faint, and that man of unholy centuries and forbidden secrets never troubled the world again. The madness out of time had subsided, and the case of Charles Dexter Ward was closed. Opening his eyes before staggering out of that room of horror, Dr. Willett saw that what he had kept in memory had not been kept amiss. There had, as he had predicted, been no need for acids. For like his accursed picture a year before, Joseph Curwen now lay scattered on the floor as a thin coating of fine bluish-grey dust.

History of the Necronomicon

(An Outline)

Original title *Al-Azif* – "azif" being the word used by the Arabs to designate that nocturnal sound (made by insects) supposed to be the howling of daemons.

Composed by Abdul Alhazred, a mad poet of Sanaa, in Yemen, who is said to have flourished during the period of the Ommiade Caliphs, circa A.D. 700. He visited the ruins of Babylon and the subterranean secrets of Memphis and spent ten years alone in the great southern desert of Arabia – (The Roba El-Khaliyeh or "empty space" of the ancients, and Dahna, or "Crimson", Desert of the modern Arabs) – which is held to be inhabited by protective evil spirits and monsters of death. Of this desert many strange and unbelievable marvels are told by those who pretend to have penetrated it. In his last years Alhazred dwelt in Damascus, where the *Necronomicon* (*Al-Azif*) was written, and of his final death or disappearance (A.D. 728) many terrible and conflicting things are told. He is said by Ebn Khallikan (12th century biographer) to have been seized by an invisible monster in broad daylight and devoured horribly before a large number of fright-frozen witnesses. Of his madness many things are told. He claimed to have seen the fabulous Item, or City of Pillars, and to have found beneath the ruins of a certain nameless desert city the shocking annals and secrets of a race older than mankind. He was only an indifferent Moslem, worshipping unknown Entities whom he called *Yog-Sothoth* and

Cthulhu.

In A.D. 950 the *Azif,* which had gained considerable though surreptitious circulation amongst the philosophers of the age, was secretly translated into Greek by Theodorus Philetas of Constantinople under the title *Necronomico*n. For a century it impelled certain experimenters to terrible attempts, when it was suppressed and burnt by the patriarch Michael. After this it was only heard of furtively, but (1228) Olaus Wormius made a Latin translation later in the Middle Ages, and the Latin text was printed twice – once in the fifteenth century in black letter (evidently in Germany) and once in the seventeenth (probably Spanish); both editions being without identifying marks, and located as to time and place by internal typographical evidence only. The work, both Latin and Greek, was banned by Pope Gregory IX in 1232 shortly after its Latin translation, which called attention to it.

The Arabic original was lost as early as Wormius' time, as indicated by his prefatory note (there is, however, a vague account of a secret copy appearing in San Francisco during the present century, but later perishing by fire), and no sight of the Greek copy – which was printed in Italy between 1500 and 1550 – has been reported since the burning of a certain Salem man's library in 1692. A translation made by Dr. Dee was never printed and exists only in fragments recovered from the original manuscript. Of the Latin texts now existing one (fifteenth century) is known to be in the British Museum under lock and key, while another (seventeenth century) is in the Bibliothèque Nationale at Paris. A seventeenth century edition is in the Widener Library at Harvard, and in the library at Miskatonic University at Arkham; also in the library of the University of Buenos Aires. Numerous other copies probably exist in secret, and a fifteenth century one is persistently rumored to form a part of the collection of a celebrated American millionaire. A still vaguer rumor credits the preservation of a sixteenth century Greek text in the Salem family of Pickman; but if it was so preserved, it vanished with the artist R. U. Pickman, who disappeared in 1926. The book is rigidly suppressed by the authorities of most countries, and by all branches of organized ecclesiasticism. Reading leads to terrible consequences. It was from rumors of this book (of which relatively few of the general public know) that R. W Chambers is said to have derived the idea of his early novel *The King in Yellow*.

CHRONOLOGY

One: *Al-Azif* written circa A.D. 730 at Damascus by Abdul Alhazred.
Two: Translated into Greek as *Necronomicon*, A.D. 950 by Theodorus Philetas.
Three: Burnt by Patriarch Michael A.D. 1050 (i.e., Greek Text... Arabic Text now lost).
Four: Olaus translates Greek into Latin, A.D. 1228.
Five: Latin and Greek editions suppressed by Gregory IX – A.D. 1232.
Six: 14..? Black letter edition printed in Germany.
Seven: 15..? Greek text printed in Italy.
Eight: 16..? Spanish translation of Latin text.